GUN THUNDER ON EAGLE RIVER

Edge Tolliver had known from that distant, tragic day when his father was found dead, that he would return to Eagle River country and solve the mystery. He soon found out that Mark Caddon, the Tumbling C boss, cut as big a swathe as ever and had even managed to wind Sheriff Moze Gall around his little finger. John Tolliver was supposed to have died accidentally by his own hand, but Edge was convinced he would eventually prove that his father had been murdered, and was ready to back up his conviction with a blazing Colt .45.

GUN THUNDER ON
EAGLE RIVER

Gun Thunder On Eagle River

by

Lee Kimber

Dales Large Print Books
Long Preston, North Yorkshire,
BD23 4ND, England.

British Library Cataloguing in Publication Data.

Kimber, Lee
   Gun thunder on Eagle River.

   A catalogue record of this book is
   available from the British Library

   ISBN   978-1-84262-506-4 pbk

First published in Great Britain in 1993 by Robert Hale Ltd.

Published in Large Print 2007 by arrangement with
Robert Hale Limited

Dales Large Print is an imprint of Library Magna Books Ltd.

Printed and bound in Great Britain by
T.J. (International) Ltd., Cornwall, PL28 8RW

ONE

Edge Tolliver broke camp at dawn in the narrow canyon where he had found the spring last night. He washed his coffee pot and scoured the bacon grease from his frying pan with a handful of sand before rinsing it and making his pack secure. A ribbon of silver was threading the east, and in a short time the land below him would be sweltering in the heat of a new day. Up here it was cold enough, with a rarity of air that pulled at Tolliver's lungs when he breathed deeply. He had never really cared much for mountain country and would be glad when he was out of it. He shifted towards the lowlands, travelling south. At midday he saw landmarks he recognized and which set his pulse to beating faster. His flat-lipped mouth thinned, grooving puckers into narrow, somewhat gaunt cheeks.

Ten years, he thought with a touch of wistfulness. A kid of sixteen in a pair of hand-me-down levis, ragged hickory shirt with the sleeves shortened to allow his skinny arms to poke through. An old hat that would never stay on his head but which kept the sun off anyhow. Mexican sandals, with his bare toes poking at the sun and the eternal dust. Spanish Ridge and the sagging buildings which his father was forever patching. His father, weather-scoured, work-bent, but infinitely patient. A determined, dogged man who never knuckled down to the vagaries of nature or the cussedness of two-legged coyotes who packed big guns strapped low on their lean hips. These scavengers chewed cigar butts as if they had been born with them between their teeth, smoked cigarettes, munched tobacco, and spat from slitted, trap-like mouths. Their eyes had the restlessness of the wind, the cold, fearsome intensity of watchful snakes.

Strangely enough though, Edge Tolliver recalled, it hadn't been their chill greetings and their gelid, mask-like features which always made his blood turn to so much ice water; it had been the way they laughed. A man ought to laugh when he was happy and feeling good with the world, when he wanted to share a joke or reminiscence with a friend or neighbour. He had no right to laugh at another man's misfortune, nor when there was nothing but hatred and derision in his heart and dark menace in the words he flung like bullets.

Tumbling C, Edge thought in this wild flood of recollection. The town of Cedarville. A fat sheriff with hairy jowls and a mole on his left jaw. Edge had no doubt about the mole being on Moze Gall's left jaw. He had studied it for long enough while he stood at his father's side and listened to them talk, his father complaining and Sheriff Gall rubbing at his whiskers and trying to avoid Jed Tolliver's hot and angry eyes.

'He's not looking at you,' he had said to his father in the way a kid might who knew nothing, or as good as nothing, of the duplicity of his elders. 'He ain't listening to a word you're saying, Paw.'

'Be still, Edgeworth,' his father had chided. And Gall, likely because the perspicacity of youth made him feel uneasy, had produced a stick of candy and extended it for Edge's grubby hand.

'You sink your teeth into that, youngster, and hold your tongue when me and your paw is palavering.'

It was something that Edge remembered well. A stick of peppermint candy to keep him quiet, to prevent him from showing the lawman's bluff for what it was. And so he had

9

listened as his father talked of Mark Caddon and the Tumbling C boss' high-handed ways. Likely Mark Caddon owned the Spanish Ridge place by now. Caddon might own the whole country around Cedarville by now. He had had ten years to pursue his ends, with no Tolliver around to get in his way.

Edge tried to push the old memories aside: they were steeped in bitterness, in tragedy. There was no proof that Mark Caddon or his foreman Gil Rimmel – or any of the rest of the Tumbling C outfit – had murdered John Tolliver. His father's death could have been an accident, just as the sheriff and the coroner had found. Tolliver had been cleaning his revolver out there by Crazy Woman Pass when the gun had gone off accidentally, blowing half of Tolliver's head away. But Edge had kept asking himself why his father had chosen such a time and place to clean his gun. The weapon and a bottle of oil and cleaning rag had been there all right when one of Homer Smith's men came on the elder Tolliver.

Edge recalled a lot of the talk from that time. There had been murmurings of rustlers on the prowl, of herds of cattle being spirited off the range. He had given it plenty of thought later, when he was able to apply a mature mind and make an assessment based on simple logic.

Old Jim Brock, a homesteader over by Eagle Butte way, had taken Edge in and looked after him for more than a year. But one day Edge slipped away, finding existence on the homestead oppressive and tiresome. He wanted to see what lay beyond the boundaries of this range, and to find out if all cowmen had been shaped in the Caddon mould.

Now Edge Tolliver was back on the Eagle River range.

The pines presently gave way to cedars. Edge had views of deer and wild turkey on the trail that snaked over wooded bench and grassy slope. He was reminded of hunting expeditions with his father. He followed a game trail for a while through the cedars and oaks, then dipped towards the lowlands, seeing aspens, June-fresh, slim and green and trembling. On out there was sage, grass; he could see cattle, hundreds of small dots: no, there must be thousands.

He felt an overpowering eagerness to read the brands the cattle wore.

When he rode down among them he saw that he had guessed correctly; the beasts were branded with a Tumbling C. It was a symbol of threat to him now, of hatred, of brooding tragedy that could assert itself again at any moment.

The cattle wallowed fatly in this wilderness of grass and wild flowers that reached up to his boots. Cedarville would be out there on his left; five miles to go now, six? North would lie the headquarters of Mark Caddon's spread, and north and west he would find what remained of the Spanish Ridge ranch. Beyond all that was Jim Brock's homestead, on the north fork of the Eagle.

The sun was a copper orb when Edge broke out of the sage at a creek to water the claybank horse. He slipped the bridle and loosened the saddle-girth. He drank and then fingered tobacco sack and papers from his shirt pocket. He was puffing at the cigarette when the thundering of hooves across the sage and grass made him wheel, anxiety running along his nerves in quick pulsations.

Two horsemen were hurrying towards him. They were well-mounted, lightly built, dark-featured men, with six-shooters swinging at their sides and rifles tucked into the scabbards below their saddle fenders. They slowed and came in to Edge at a walk, left hands holding reins high, right hands free and dangling with a significance that caused Edge's mouth to go tight and dry.

He essayed a cool smile and pushed his hat up from his brow. 'Howdy, gents,' he greeted. 'Sure is nice to see men critters for a change.'

'That a fact?' The speaker gave his companion a look that was a mixture of amusement and contempt. Both men relaxed and leaned their bodies forward, the better to examine the tall, craggy-jawed stranger. 'You're new to these parts, ain't you?'

'You could put it that way, I guess,' Edge replied easily.

'But you don't know where you are?'

Edge puffed for a minute while he appeared to consider that. He gestured. 'I take it Cedarville is over thataway?'

'Say, you're real sharp, mister! If you climb on to your horse this minute and start riding, you'll reach Cedarville when you see it. How about that?'

His companion laughed without humour. They were a humourless pair, these two. They laughed in a way that was not a laugh at all. Edge dipped his head in meagre acknowledgement.

'Guess I'll be heading there shortly,' he said.

'No, pilgrim,' was the stony, inflexible response. 'You'll be heading there right now. You're on land that belongs to Tumbling C, and what with cow-thieves and suchlike making life hard for everybody, we don't cotton to strangers – drifters or otherwise.'

Edge's mouth bent at the corners. 'Say, mister, that's about as close to a speech as I ever heard. So you're taking me for a rustler?' His tone hardened perceptibly.

The former speaker shot a quick glance at his friend. The planes of his long-jawed face flattened. 'Didn't say that at all. But we got a job to do and we do it. So how about saving everybody a heap of trouble and getting on your way?'

'When I'm good and ready.' Edge's voice had hit rock bottom now. It seemed only yesterday when Mark Caddon and Gil Rimmel hammered up to the ranch-house on Spanish Ridge and spoke harshly to his father. This was the manner of speaking they used, this the same over-riding boldness and brash assertiveness. Their warning could ring in his brain at any moment he wished to call it up.

You're not wanted here, Tolliver. Why don't you stop behaving stupid? Why don't you take your brat and find some place else to raise cows and chickens?

14

The long-jawed gentleman was speaking again. His chin jutted with a growing belligerence. He kept glancing at his friend, throwing him knowing, covert winks. 'I guess you didn't hear me right, *hombre*. Or maybe you're dimmer than I figured. What's the matter with taking a friendly tip that could save you a platterful of grief?'

While the man talked, his right hand travelled along his flank to where his six-shooter nestled. Edge wondered if the Caddon man would go ahead and use it if he thought he should. But Edge Tolliver had found out how to handle situations such as this. As soon as you smelled a threat you took the initiative.

Edge went for his own gun.

The movement was a blurred dipping of fingers that resembled striking talons. Then the fingers became a fist that held a walnut-stocked .45 levelled steadily and already cocked.

'Hey, what's this?'

'Just what you see,' Edge drawled. 'A Mr Sam Colt. It shoots real fast. But heck, you've got one of your own there on your leg...'

'Let's go, Cash,' the other Caddon rider urged tautly.

15

'In a minute, Pinto. Stranger, you just made a terrible bad move. You'd better listen to a word of advice–'

'Keep it.'

'You'll get it anyhow, mister,' Cash snarled. 'Might save your fool hide if you listen to it. If you're heading for Cedarville, make it a short stop. Air around there wouldn't agree with a fella like you.'

'If that's the best you can do I'd say it's time to turn your horse's tail to me,' Edge came back tartly.

'Of all the damn nerve...' Pinto exploded.

'Raise dust, gents.' Edge's tone was uncompromising. He raised the bore of his revolver so that it centred on Pinto's chest, just where the neck of his shirt opened.

'Do you know who you're bucking, you lunkhead?' Cash roared.

'Two mangy coyotes? Sure, I do. And they're going to be plenty dead coyotes if they don't fan the breeze out of here.'

'Who are you, mister? Doesn't matter anyhow. You won't live to see the sun go down.'

Edge squeezed trigger and his bullet whined past Cash's head. He yelped in terror and almost fell out of his saddle. Pinto's hatchet face had gone ashen. Their horses plunged and reared. Cash loped out first, whirling his mount with a wicked thrust of spurs that sent it racing through the sage. Pinto shouted something at Tolliver and went after his companion. Edge watched with amusement until they had gone from view.

His face sobered somewhat as uneasiness took over. He had planned on making an unobtrusive return to this country, giving himself time to look around and see how things had changed since he had left as a callow sixteen-year-old to view the other side of those eastern New Mexico hills. Instead, he had run into a couple of Caddon's riders almost straight off, been threatened by them, and in turn had thrown a scare into the pair called Pinto and Cash.

It wasn't a good start, but it couldn't be helped. At least he had found out that the same overbearing riders ranged the Eagle River country. Rustling – that ubiquitous cattle country disease – was as rife as ever.

Edge mounted and cut out for the Cedarville trail. He viewed this mighty sprawl of land with distrust now. He could not be sure what the Caddon men would do after they had licked their sores and taken stock. They were not the type to bend to the will of a nervy drifter, and if they had failed to impress him on the need to keep moving they would resort to more subtle and deadlier tactics.

At length he found himself riding through a lush valley with a watercourse on his right and a cluster of low hills on his left. Up there were aspens and oaks, contriving a ragged screen against the sky. In a short while he would reach Cedarville, where he would spend a little time picking up news. Afterwards he would pay a call on old Jim Brock – if Jim was still alive and on his homestead, that was. And he had a hankering to put his horse through the grass that covered Spanish Ridge. Springtime was fine out there, with summer making its surge towards full ripeness. The hills would be colourful with wild flowers; the pools and streams would be running with trout. Most of all, perhaps, he wanted to see the old house again, if it was still standing.

The rifle shot from the timberline jarred him back to the moment. The bullet whistled through the air, mere inches from the claybank's head. The horse reared and spun as another shot roared out; this time the bullet came closer to Edge. He sent his horse racing out on the right, making for the stream and a stand of cottonwoods on the far bank.

Two rifles barked spitefully now, and Edge was sweating by the time he splashed through the stream and burst in among the trees.

He fought the frightened claybank to a standstill, dismounted, and secured the reins to a sapling. He tugged his Winchester free and moved to the border of the trees to scan the hills up yonder.

He triggered immediately on glimpsing a movement, then waited for reaction. He saw a loose horse for a few seconds, but he held his fire. The horse went from sight, and on the same instant another bullet flailed the thicket where he crouched. Edge sent off two spaced shots in reply.

He had no doubt that the ambushers were the Caddon men, Cash and Pinto. As he had judged, they had decided to find some way of turning the tables on the stranger and reinstating their own rules. They would be reluctant to go home to Mark Caddon and admit they had been bested by a drifter who had nothing to recommend him but a slick draw.

There was a period of silence that was broken only by the croak of a raven in the high branches. The claybank nickered at his back. Edge wondered if there was any way the Caddon pair might work in behind him to try and take him by surprise. He decided, however, that this would be virtually impossible.

Later still, he fancied he glimpsed a horse bobbing into a grassy fold in the hills, but he couldn't be sure. It was simply a blur of movement that could have been a deer. The sun slipped across the sky and the heat grew stronger, and finally Edge was forced to consider that Cash and Pinto must have pulled out. After all, they knew he was making for Cedarville, and setting up a trap in town might suit their purpose better.

Finally he took his horse into the open and mounted. He would be in plain view of the ambushers if they were still located up yonder. But nothing happened. The half-expected shot never came. Edge rode for several miles before letting the tension generated by expectancy fall away. All the same, he kept scanning the land to right and left, kept searching his back trail. But the time passed and the miles fell away under the hooves of his claybank horse, and then he topped out a ridge and saw the outlines of the town of Cedarville limned against the blue sky.

TWO

In a way it was the town he remembered and yet in another way it seemed a different place entirely. The Street he had imagined to be so long and so wide now appeared to his man's eyes to have lessened in width and length. The buildings that flanked the dusty road had surely shrunk in stature and importance. The stores, offices and residential buildings – like everything else that waged a continuous fight against the ravages of time and weather – bore ample witness to how the battle would eventually be decided.

Roof shakes had worked loose, wooden pillars that had once seemed so stable and enduring were withering and beginning to sag. The hotel and most of the saloons needed paint, as did many of the stores. Here and there, where adobes had stood, were spaces like missing teeth in an ageing mouth.

Still, business appeared to be pretty good, Edge noted. The racks fronting stores and saloon were lined with horses. Freight wagons rocked through the yellow dust.

Women in calico and gingham, with sun-bonnets held to their chins with ribbons, mingled with cowhands, teamsters and miners from the silver workings to the south. All in all, it was a colourful – almost exhilarating – sight, what with the bright clothing worn by the women and the constant shifting of movement and the variety of noises.

A hammer clanged from the wide entrance to a blacksmith's forge. Edge glimpsed a brawny man, skin sleek and brown in the gloom, great muscles rippling as he wielded his hammer. A couple of loafers stood about the gateway; in the forge a man was holding a couple of horses in readiness. Edge remembered standing, wide-eyed, in that very gateway while his father had a horse shod. Ed Riley was as hefty and as handsome as ever, but the showering of sparks and the winking of the fire gave the returned stranger a view of black hair that had begun to turn grey. Edge went on past, holding his claybank to a walk while his gaze sought eagerly for other sights he wished to recall and savour.

The meeting with the men Pinto and Cash along the trail had almost slipped his mind at this juncture. But when he drew level with Willie Moon's saloon and saw three fine horses with their owners hitching reins he frowned, picking out the stooped frame of another Caddon rider, Pritch Stevens.

Pritch's face was as bleak as ever, thinner, more pinched around the mouth and nostrils. The narrow, close-set eyes touched the stranger and held for an instant, and Edge wondered if the foxy brain would make a successful journey into the past. But there was no sign of recognition on the cowhand's features. Stevens looked on along the street before speaking to his companions from the side of his mouth. The characteristic was all too sharply etched on Edge's memory. Pritch Stevens was furtive, cunning, small-minded and soured against all mankind. Rumour always had it that Pritch had shot up a family of homesteaders out at Aspen Canyon, killing the father and wounding the mother of four children. But that was before Edge Tolliver's time, and he had often wondered if the story were true.

Edge drew closer to the livery barn and stables that now occupied the space separating Silver's Hotel from Dawson's Mercantile. A clattering of hooves from the opposite end of the street claimed his attention, and he watched while four horsemen came closer. He caught his breath on recognizing the tall, square-shouldered man in the lead.

This was Mark Caddon himself, heavy and ponderous, big head rolling this way and that on his thick bull neck. Caddon would be about fifty now, Edge reckoned, but not a whit of change could he detect in this man he had grown to fear and detest with all the ardour of youth. His foreman, Gil Rimmel, rode on Caddon's left flank, whipcord tough as always, tall and straight in the saddle, pale blue eyes staring fixedly at something discernible to no one else. Edge could not recall the other two men, but they bore that stamp of cruelty and ruthlessness that ran like a swollen, rotten root through everything pertaining to Tumbling C.

Edge had brought his mount to a halt. He could feel cold sweat coming to his brow and a coiling of sickness gathered in his stomach. It was a moment, too, when the scales finally fell from his eyes, and he knew as surely as the sun was hanging in the sky that Mark Caddon or some of his crew had done away with his father.

The sensation was brief, and he felt foolish immediately afterwards. He was blaming the Tumbling C men because they had harassed his father, because they had never let up in their efforts to drive the Tollivers from their land.

Caddon's restless eyes raked Edge briefly and passed on with no glimmer of recognition – or interest, come to that. Still, why should a man like Caddon remember Edge Tolliver, the brat who always clung to his father's side when he called at Spanish Ridge? And why should Caddon worry even if he did find out that Edge was back on his home ground?

More horses pounded along the road, and Edge saw four cowhands with a fifth rider hemmed in the centre, this one with hair awry and shirt sleeves torn. His wrists were bound in front of him. People on the street halted to stare. Men emerged from saloons and formed little knots. Women vacated the sidewalks, grabbing their children as they went. A whisper lifted in the suddenly quiet street and ran like a breeze among aspen leaves.

'They've caught one of the rustlers,' a storekeeper grunted. 'Caddon's men have caught a rustler...'

'Figure it'll be another hanging?'

'Hell yes! Only way to stamp it out. Sheriff Gall's all for wiping the rustlers out. Saves time and money.'

A few others joined the group and, listening to them, the blood ran cold in

25

Edge's veins. Was this what things had come to since he'd been gone? Had Mark Caddon become a complete law unto himself, filling the roles of judge, jury and executioner?

The Caddon riders had halted on up at the plaza. Edge twisted his claybank in the road and retraced his way through the dust. A crowd was gathering at the front of Needham's grain store. A circle formed around the men who had brought the prisoner in. The prisoner himself fascinated Edge in a strange way. He was about his own age, straight-backed and upright in his saddle. His face was as pale as death but his lips were compressed stubbornly and there was an appealing boldness in the eyes that swept his captors.

Mark Caddon was off his horse by then, and Edge watched as Sheriff Moze Gall pushed his way into the circle.

'All right, folks, all right!' Gall protested in a crackling voice. 'Let's stand back a bit so everybody can get some air.' There was revolting obsequiousness in his manner as he turned to the cattle baron. 'So you managed to grab another one of them, Mr Caddon?'

'What does it look like?' Caddon retorted. His tone was flat and showed Edge, as

26

nothing else could, how the law was being treated with blatant contempt.

Silence fell again as Caddon cleared his throat. It was expected that he make some kind of speech. Plainly Caddon's was the voice of whatever brand of law and order existed around these parts. But the cowman just gestured at the prisoner, rolling his head this way and that as if to emphasise the gravity of the situation.

'Where did you catch him, Mark?' the sheriff wanted to know, striving to exert some authority. 'Isn't that a nester that lives over there beyond Spanish Ridge?'

'Course he is.'

Edge had dismounted. He held his horse on close rein. His spine tingled at the mention of Spanish Ridge and he examined the features of the captive more closely. The man was a stranger to him. The face sweated a little: it was clean-cut, square-jawed. The eyes were twin pools of grey-green fire. An honest face, if Edge Tolliver knew anything at all about human nature. If this man had been branded a rustler, where was the proof to back up the charge?

'His name's Rufe Gates,' Mark Caddon was saying. 'My men have been watching him for about a year. You all know how I've been losing stock from that end of the range, and you know how the other cattlemen out there are being preyed on by these parasites. I've complained to the sheriff here often enough.'

'That you have,' Moze Gall agreed. 'But did you get this man cold, Mark? Can you and your men stand up and say they actually saw Gates stealing your cattle?'

Caddon's stare was laced with bitterness. 'We got him cold all right. You tell him, Gil.'

The foreman coughed as if something had become stuck in his throat. He appeared to have difficulty looking the sheriff straight in the eye. 'Buck Masters and me was taking a look at the west end of the range early this morning–'

'That would've been over Spanish Ridge way.' Gall broke in as if he wished to get this point clear so that no one could dispute the claim afterwards.

'That's right,' Rimmel nodded. 'We were coming out of a coulee when Buck spotted this gent driving half a dozen head of our beef. It was the sort of chance we'd been waiting for, and–'

'You're a damned liar, Rimmel!' Rufe Gates erupted.

A hush held the gathering for the space of

ten seconds. Edge Tolliver's horse nickered at his back. The claybank was not used to crowds and loud, bickering voices. Moze Gall raised a hand.

'Gates, you're not helping your case by getting on like this,' he declared sententiously. 'Go ahead, Gil.'

'Well, there's nothing much else to it, Sheriff. We went after this jasper and caught him.'

'What did he say about the cows?' Gall pressed.

'They were steers,' Rimmel explained. 'He said he wasn't stealing them.'

'What about it, Gates?' the sheriff challenged the homesteader.

'I wasn't after their cattle,' Gates protested. 'I wouldn't touch anything that belonged to Caddon or his neighbours. Why should I? Even if I wanted to be a thief I couldn't afford to be. I've got a wife depending on me, a kid...'

'Pity you didn't think of them before you started stealing,' Mark Caddon flung at him.

'You know this is just a farce,' the homesteader retorted. 'You want me out of the way. You can't bear to see anything on the range that doesn't bear your brand. You can hardly stand your own neighbours, and if the truth were known–'

'That'll do,' Moze Gall rapped at him. 'It's easy flinging dirt when you're sitting on a heap of it yourself.'

'No, it won't do, Sheriff,' Rufe Gates objected. 'I want these people to hear the truth about what's going on on this range. Cattle are being stolen, sure, but not in half-dozens like Rimmel would have you believe. They're being stolen in scores, hundreds!'

'Listen to that rat squeak,' one of the Caddon men sneered.

'Just listen to me!' Gates insisted. 'Ask Art Cox. Ask Gard Miller. One or two rustlers couldn't make such big cuts. It would take a big crew to do it. A crew that can ride anywhere they like and do anything they like. *Ask Mark Caddon there about it!*'

Rufe Gates' voice rose to a high pitch, broke with emotion. He looked around for some kind of help, for some form of encouragement, even a little understanding. He was met by a ring of tight faces, some indifferent, some doubtful, some plain hostile.

Mark Caddon's laugh boomed like a cracked bell, harsh with contempt for every word that Gates had spoken. He shrugged, rolled his big head on his thick neck, spread his hands to the gathering.

'I guess you folks can see what we have to put up with out there. We're surrounded by thieves, by liars. They're nothing but pests, and there's only one way to deal with them.'

'I reckon it's a plain enough case,' Sheriff Gall agreed. His tone reeked with hypocrisy. 'And I'm glad you brought everything out into the open so the good people of this town can hear and judge for themselves.'

'Do I have to say any more then, Sheriff?' Caddon queried. 'Or does my word still hold good?'

'Mr Caddon, we all know you and respect you as a rancher with sound ethics and un-questionable morals,' Gall declared loudly. 'Why, without men like you, what would we have here – a desert, that's what! Wild men roaming at will as they used to. There couldn't be a town like Cedarville without cattlemen like you and your neighbours. And if the law can't back you up in your times of trial, then I say it's time the law ceased to exist altogether as a recognized formal force. Do we let the wolf and the coyote have the calf? Do we let a man prey on his brother without fear of reprisal and retribution...'

'Let the sand reclaim the place where we

lay our heads down at night,' a man beside Edge muttered with savage relish. And Edge could scarcely believe his ears when the lawman recited those very words.

The man grinned lopsidedly. 'You ain't heard this speech before? One of Moze's favourites. He read it from a book he got some place.'

Edge was aware of a quickening of pulse-beat, of a kindling of wrath in the pit of his stomach that threatened to become a consuming furnace. He bit his lip, choking back a hard challenge. The hapless victim seated on the restive horse had his chin resting on his chest now. He was being forced to accept the inevitable.

Suddenly a stir broke out on the fringe of the crowd.

Edge heard a young voice shouting something. He glimpsed a youngster, then a girl who was trying to restrain the boy. The youth pushed his way through the gathering, his voice cracking with feeling.

'You let Mr Gates be!' he shouted. 'He ain't done nothing...'

'Vern!' the girl called. 'Vern, come back here.'

'Somebody's got to help Rufe, Sis,' the boy protested. 'We're his friends, ain't we?'

He had reached the edge of the clearing, and Mark Caddon barked an order at one of his men. The cowhand strode forward and gripped the boy's arm.

'Better shut your mouth, sonny.'

The boy wriggled, tried to kick the cowboy's ankles. 'Rufe, do you hear me?' he yelled. 'We're right with you, Rufe.'

'I know you are, Vern.' A tide of colour lifted in Rufe Gates' pale cheeks. 'But you mustn't make trouble for Barbie.'

'But they aim to hang you, damn it!'

'Vern!'

'But they are, Sis. They done hung Jubal Prescott. Jubal never done nothing and neither did Rufe.'

Moze Gall thrust himself into the circle. 'Take him away,' he barked. 'Another word out of you, kid, and I'll beat the ears off'n your head.'

The boy was dragged off, still protesting, still kicking at anything within range of his feet. Edge looked at the girl now, noting the clean-cut profile, the mass of honey-gold hair that tumbled about her shoulders. Then he swung to where men were closing in on Rufe Gates.

Somebody was up yonder at the grain hoist, and a rope was being paid down. A noose dangled terrifyingly at the end of it. Edge gritted his teeth, letting his attention range over the gathering. Surely these people would not permit this travesty of justice to run its course? There were bound to be men here who sympathised with the homesteader, who believed that, at the very least, he deserved a proper trial with a judge, jury and appropriate lawyers.

It appeared, however, that this was not the case. Either everyone believed Rufe Gates to be a rustler or they were too frightened to tangle with Mark Caddon and the creature who called himself a sheriff.

The girl shouted in a thin scream. 'This is murder!'

'Get it over with,' Mark Caddon roared.

The noose was in place and the self-elected executioner prepared to switch the horse from under him.

'Hold it right there,' Edge Tolliver called. 'Man who makes that horse jump is dead...'

THREE

Everyone seemed to freeze where they stood. Then all eyes switched to the tall man beside the claybank horse. This stranger in their midst had a revolver gripped firmly in his fingers and the muzzle was tilted squarely on the Caddon man who had appointed himself the executioner of Rufe Gates. A ripple of sound ran over the gathering, quickened, gathered volume. It was left to Sheriff Moze Gall to challenge Edge Tolliver.

'Who in blazes are you, mister? This is no mix of yours. Put that gun up. Put it up, I tell you!'

'Soon as you release that man,' Edge drawled. 'He's no rustler.'

'What! How do you know who he is or what he is? You're sure sticking your neck out, stranger.'

'I want to know how you come to the conclusion he's a rustler,' Edge countered. He continued to point the gun at the Caddon rider. The crowd began to part and fall back so that he was soon in full view of

35

the sheriff and the Caddon crew. Rufe Gates stared as if he found it hard to believe the evidence of his eyes. The last thing he had expected was that someone would speak up for him, much less turn a gun on the Tumbling C faction on his behalf.

'You heard the evidence Mr Caddon's foreman put forward,' Moze Gall retorted. The sheriff was still off balance; an interruption of this nature was the last thing he had expected. 'Anyhow,' he went on blusteringly, 'you've no right to poke your nose in where it doesn't concern you.'

'It concerns me,' Edge spat. 'Just as it ought to concern every right-thinking member of this community. I've seen some half-baked towns, but this one beats them all. Not a voice to speak out for the homesteader but a kid and a girl!' Some of Edge's pent-up anger spilled into his voice. His eyes shifted to the owner of the Tumbling C, noted the fury that pulsed into Mark Caddon's heavy-jowled face. Caddon's men had ranged themselves on either side of their boss and were ready to act if he gave the order. 'This man deserves a fair trial by a judge and jury–'

'He deserves nothing.' Caddon had found his voice. He took a couple of steps that put him between Edge and his mounted prisoner. 'You'd be advised to pull your horns in, friend. Put that gun away and ride on out of town.'

'Stand aside,' Edge said coolly.

'I'm standing right here.' The eyes challenging Edge were baleful, hot with a churning hatred. Edge wondered how far he could push the cattleman before he called on his dogs to bite.

'If you don't stand aside I'll drill you,' Edge told him. 'I mean it, mister.'

Their glances fused in a battle of wills for a few more seconds. Then Edge glimpsed a blur of movement on his right as one of Caddon's men went for his gun. Tolliver switched his Colt and triggered. The cowhand screamed in agony as a bullet shattered his arm and flung him round in a driving circle. He finished up squirming in the dust. Mark Caddon started to draw, changed his mind swiftly, and fell back a couple of paces. Edge fanned the bunch with his six-shooter.

'Next one to try a sneak shot will get his head blown off,' he warned.

'Stranger, you're sure bucking big trouble,' Moze Gall panted. 'You'd better heed Mark's advice and clear out of here mighty sudden.'

'When I'm good and ready,' Edge replied

thinly. 'A man who hasn't the guts to rod the law shouldn't talk so much.'

'Why, you nervy–'

'Don't do anything foolish, Mr Gall. Far as I'm concerned, that tin badge don't mean a damn thing. Not with you behind it anyway.'

The scathing regard that lingered briefly on the lawman served to melt the remnants of his courage. He darted a look at Mark Caddon, but the cowman was watching Edge Tolliver.

'Now,' Edge said to the man who had been about to switch the homesteader's horse from under him, 'release your prisoner.'

'Release him! But we got to–'

'You heard me, fella.'

The crowd watched tensely while the ropes that pinioned Rufe Gates's wrists were cut. The girl with the honey-gold hair appeared with the youngster called Vern. They hurried forward to help the home-steader dismount. On the ground, Gates stood unsteadily for a moment, looking at the circle of still faces.

'Are you all right, Rufe?' the dark-haired youngster in cotton shirt and patched levis asked him.

'I'm fine, Vern.'

Gates shuffled over to Edge Tolliver then. He was nervous and confused, but he mustered a weak smile. 'Thanks for the help, mister. But you're just wasting your time. They'll come after me again. It's that kind of country.'

'If it's got so bad why don't you pack up and leave?' Edge suggested.

'It's what they want me to do. But I'm not going to run. I never learned that habit and I'm not starting now.'

Gates extended his hand and Edge took it. The crowd had started to break up, leaving the Tumbling C men standing around in a loose group. Sheriff Gall had disappeared altogether. It was as if everyone wanted to get off the street just then, leaving the stage to Tolliver, Rufe Gates, and the boy and girl who had retreated to the sidewalk. They stood with their backs against the wall of a store. As the citizens of Cedarville saw it, there was only one way this confrontation could end – in gunfire.

No guns were unlimbered, however. Edge took his horse and went along the Street, the homesteader leading his own horse beside him. A couple of Caddon's cowhands began to follow the two men, but Mark Caddon brought them to heel.

'Take it easy,' he grunted. 'There's no hurry.'

'But, hell, Boss, that gent made us look like a lot of scared fools. We'll never live it down.'

'Don't worry, Johnny,' Caddon told him with a warped grin. 'We'll live it down. If we'd cut loose just then we might have turned people against us. We'd be branded roughnecks and killers. Well, we've shown we're men of tolerance and patience. You heard what that bird Gates said? He doesn't intend to run. Means we have all the time there is to settle the score.'

'What about the stranger?' another of the group demanded. 'Figure he's going to hang around?'

Caddon didn't answer immediately. He was watching the girl, Barbie Wilson, and her young brother talking with Gates and the stranger. They were close to the gateway leading to the livery. Gates shook hands with the stranger once more before the tall man disappeared inside.

'He's going to get a feed for his horse,' Caddon surmised reflectively. 'It could be that he aims to stop over for a spell.' He turned to his foreman. 'You ever see that bird anywhere before, Gil?'

Gil Rimmel thought for a while, thrust his fingers under his sweatband and scratched. He shook his head finally. 'Can't say I have. But he sure ain't afraid of trouble.'

Caddon nodded in an abstracted fashion. It seemed to him that some chord in his memory had been plucked by the appearance of the newcomer. In some odd way that craggy-jawed face was vaguely familiar. He shrugged, deciding he would think about it later.

'You go after Jase to the doc's place, Gil. See if his wing is badly hurt. All right, men ... I'll see the rest of you later across in Moon's saloon.'

Caddon took his horse down the street until he was on a level with the timber and brick building that housed Moze Gall's office and the jail block. He dismounted and stood for a little while, looking around him. He knew that many eyes continued to watch him curiously. His reputation was such that the townspeople expected him to bring the brash stranger to heel at the first opportunity.

No doubt they believed Mark Caddon had taken a weighty kick to the stomach, that one man calling his bluff was a bitter pill for him to swallow. A sour smile touched the corners

41

of his mouth without managing to reach his eyes. Caddon cared little for the people in this town. They knew him for what he was and respected him for what he was – a tough, untiring worker who had most of the cattle country out there held snugly in the palm of his hand. And that same hand was big enough to give this damned town a hard squeeze if he chose to apply real pressure...

Moze Gall was seated at his desk when Caddon went into the office. Judging by the glum expression on the lawman's face, Gall had been expecting the visit. He fingered his beard nervously.

'What do you want me to do?' he asked in a flat voice. 'Arrest him and throw him into a cell to cool off?'

A flicker of contempt crossed Caddon's eyes, vanished. 'Who are you talking about Moze – Rufe Gates or the stranger who saved his neck?'

'Hell, the stranger, of course.' Gall's skin darkened. Resentment smouldered briefly. 'Do you think I'm scared of him?'

'Are you?' Caddon countered. But then, deciding that diplomacy was the better course: 'Forget it. Nobody's saying you're scared, Moze. Simmer down. But it doesn't look good when a man you've never seen before can ride into town and poke a gun at you. That's just how it looked, Moze.'

A nerve jumped high up on the lawman's left cheek. A retort sprang to his lips but he stifled it. 'Is – is he still in town?'

'Saw him at the livery.'

'He's staying then.' Gall's efforts to hide his fear were not entirely successful. Nevertheless he heaved himself to his feet and took a rifle from the rack against the wall.

Caddon frowned as he watched. 'Where are you going, Moze?'

'To get him.'

Caddon laughed with sour humour and the sheriff glared at him, showing a flash of spirit. 'You think I'm too scared to do it, don't you, Mark? I've skulked about this town for so long like a Tumbling C lapdog that folks think I can't make a move unless you give me an order...'

'Hold your tongue, you fool,' Caddon snapped contemptuously.

For a moment it appeared that Moze Gall would continue his bitter harangue, but then his shoulders slumped and the fire died out of his eyes, leaving them dull and lifeless.

'What's the use?' he gritted. 'Why should I stick my neck out when nobody cares a curse?'

Caddon placed a hand on his shoulder. 'Now you're talking sense, Moze. Why go throwing your weight around on account of an upstart stranger?'

'But you can see the danger,' Gall said hoarsely. 'He made me look bad in front of everybody. He made your boys look bad, too. If I let him run wild, folks will start wondering. I could end up being no more than a sick joke in the territory.'

'It won't come to that,' the cowman assured him. 'If he stops off for an hour or so, well and good. If he decides to hang around and go on pulling the dog's tail, then something will have to be done about him.'

'Mark, was – was it true what Gil Rimmel said? Did he really catch Rufe Gates stealing cattle? I wouldn't stand for that kind of business, you know.'

Caddon's jaw hardened. 'You doubt what my men say? Haven't we kept this range pretty clean for you, done a lot of the dirty work for you?'

'Sure, I understand. But this stealing's getting out of hand. Gard Miller lost seventy or eighty steers a couple of weeks ago. I've got to catch these damn cow-thieves one way or another.'

'Now you're beginning to see things my

way,' Caddon purred. 'I told you before that the rope's the only sure-fire cure. And I'm telling you here and now, Moze, if Gates doesn't clear out of the country he's going to get his neck stretched.'

Caddon left the lawman on that note. He headed down the street and was about to go into Moon's saloon when he spotted two of his riders coming through the dust.

'Hold on, Boss...'

'Hello, Pinto,' Caddon greeted peevishly when Gahan and Cash Mayne had drawn level. 'What's the matter?'

The cowhands dismounted and tied their horses at the rail. Pinto Gahan looked excited about something. 'Did you notice a stranger around town lately?' he wanted to know. 'Big fella on a claybank nag?'

Caddon's mouth tightened. 'He busted up our lynching bee at the grain store.'

'The hell you say! Where is he about now?'

'Hold on, damn it,' their boss rasped. 'Tell me what happened.'

Gahan explained how they had come on the stranger on their grass, and how he had reacted when they ordered him to keep moving. Mark Caddon's frown deepened when Pinto related how they had lain up in the trees to ambush Tolliver.

'That was a bad move for sure,' he grunted. 'Tell me, Pinto, did this gent strike you as odd in any way?'

'You mean did I ever see him before?'

'Did you?'

Gahan shook his head. When Caddon repeated his question to Cash Mayne he received the same response. 'What's on your mind?' Pinto queried.

'Well, I've a strange hunch that I've run across him somewhere. Can't put a finger on the time or place. Quite a little while ago, I'd say. But when?' Caddon pursed his thick lips. His head rolled.

'Is he in town?' Pinto pressed.

'He's here. But let him be for the time being. I've a feeling he won a lot of sympathy from that damn crowd when he made Pete release Gates. Killing him right now might start something we couldn't live down. I don't like the way the sheriff's behaving either. He'd turn us in if he had a shred of evidence against us.'

Cash Mayne nodded glumly. 'But suppose the stranger makes a habit of messing up our plans?'

'He'll not live that long.' Caddon shrugged, his smile no more than a narrowing of cold eyes. He scanned the street for sign of the newcomer, but Edge Tolliver was not to be seen. Caddon jerked his head. 'Come on in here and I'll buy you boys a drink.'

His horse taken care of, Edge Tolliver made his way towards one of the smaller saloons along the main drag. He guessed that the Tumbling C men were up yonder at Moon's place, discussing his interference in their business and trying to decide the best way of putting him out of action. It occurred to him that he might have acted too hastily at the grain store. After all, a hanging was a serious affair, and a man who interfered at the critical moment would not be forgiven by those bent on dealing out their own brand of justice.

Edge supposed that, had he really been a stranger to these parts, he might have kept himself to himself and let the hanging go ahead. It was because of Tumbling C's involvement that he had butted in. But no, he told himself, he must be honest about the whole thing. There was something terribly wrong in hanging any man without a proper trial. And, furthermore, he was convinced that Rufe Gates was not a rustler.

He shouldered into a saloon and ordered a drink at the dingy bar. His thoughts switched from Rufe Gates and the men bent on hanging him to the boy called Vern and his sister. The girl had struck him as being honest and sincere. She was Gates' neighbour, and she had been so sure he was getting a raw deal that she and her brother had come to town to speak in his defence.

Edge had been surprised to learn that the Wilsons were living on the old Tolliver place at Spanish Ridge. The girl's parting words came back to him. *'If you need a job I would like to hire you. I could do with a couple of riders, but everyone is too scared to work for an outfit that has been threatened by Tumbling C.'*

He had neglected to give them his name. But he had promised Barbie Wilson to call at Spanish Ridge and let her know what he decided.

He drank another beer, and was about to leave when his eyes flickered to the back-bar mirror. The swing doors had been pushed open and Sheriff Moze Gall was shouldering through.

FOUR

The sheriff didn't move directly to the counter; instead, he stood with the doors flapping at his back, scanning the customers. Presently he looked squarely at the mirror and his eyes clashed with Edge Tolliver's.

Edge finished his drink and produced cigarette makings. He watched the fat man with the beard shifting on over the floor, and turned slightly so that Gall could not surprise him with a drawn gun.

'Hello, Sheriff.'

'So you're still in town, eh?'

'That's where I am.'

The lawman placed his elbows on the bar and signalled to the bartender.

'Usual, Mr Gall?'

'Just a beer, Sime, like this bird was drinking.'

The beer was slid out, and Moze Gall insisted on paying in spite of Sime's dismissive wave of the hand. He cuffed his mouth before taking a mouthful of beer, then cuffed it again, smacking his lips. Edge found himself staring at the mole on his left cheek.

Watching him this way, it was like going back ten years to the ranch on Spanish Ridge. Memories swamped him, filling his ears with familiar voices, the sounds of his boyhood.

A terrible wrath took hold of him as he stood there watching the thick-bellied star-packer. Gall was just as ineffectual as ever, as weak as ever. Had he done his duty all those years ago, John Tolliver might still be alive, and the Spanish Ridge ranch might be thriving. Edge Tolliver might never have gone away.

'Guess you ain't a very good listener, mister,' Gall observed after another mouthful of beer. He kept his eyes averted, pretending to be looking at the bartender. He had a thin, bogus smile at his lips. It was intended to show everyone that he was perfectly capable of handling this upstart newcomer.

'What do you want me to listen to?' Edge queried.

'I told you earlier, buster. I don't make a habit of repeating myself.'

Edge stared at him until Gall was obliged to meet his gaze. 'You advised me to leave town. How come you're so anxious to get rid of me?'

'I just want to spare you a lot of grief.'

'The sort of grief Mark Caddon dishes out?'

'That's the truth, buster, and don't you forget it.'

'Caddon's a real big wheel hereabouts, isn't he? Everybody jumps when he's around. Do you jump as well, Mr Gall?'

'I don't jump for anybody, mister. And you'd better mind your tongue.' Gall finished his beer, cuffed his beard. The bartender hovered, but he shook his head. He indicated a table over by the wall. 'Let's sit for a minute.'

'Why not? Sure you won't have another drink?'

Gall demurred, and Edge took another schooner of beer over to the table where the fat man had seated himself. Moze Gall sighed, knocked his hat to the crown of his head. He placed a stogie between lips that were almost hidden by the dark beard, struck a match and puffed. He considered Edge Tolliver's slightly amused expression through a cloud of smoke.

'I ought to run you in for what you did today,' he said in conversational fashion. 'You acted real high-handed, and you put me in a bad light with all those folks watching.'

'Never intended putting you in a bad light. Will you tell me something, Sheriff?'

'If I can.' He looked dubious, suspicious.

'Did Mark Caddon send you after me?' Edge asked him. 'Because if he did he's in for a—'

'Nobody sends me anywhere,' Gall interrupted. 'I'm just giving you fair warning. Nobody stamps on Caddon's toes the way you did and gets away with it. Maybe you figure you tweaked his tail some, but you didn't. You're mistaken if you think you did. And if nobody has told you yet, Caddon happens to be the biggest rancher in this part of the country.'

'Orneriest too, I'd say,' was Edge's blithe rejoinder.

His smile served to incense the other. 'All right, friend. Let me put it this way then: if you don't light a fast shuck out of this town you're as good as dead.'

Edge's eyes widened in affected surprise. 'You mean I can't call on you for protection?'

'My job is to protect the innocent, mister. I've no time to waste on meddlers and troublemakers.'

'So who do you protect?' Edge flashed back. 'That poor critter who was about to be sent to Hades with a rope around his neck? And what about John Tolliver who was shot to death...?'

Too late he realized what he had said. The words got mangled up in his teeth and he drew a hard breath. Moze Gall's face went very pale.

'What do you know about John Tolliver?' he demanded thickly. 'Just what in hell are you talking about?'

'I happened to hear how he was killed. He was murdered out at Crazy Woman Pass.'

'Murdered!' Gall echoed. 'Do you know what you're saying? John Tolliver killed himself accidentally. His gun went off when he was cleaning it.'

'The story I heard was different,' Edge countered.

'Who told you this story?' Gall leaned forward on his elbows. His eyes bored into the man opposite him.

'Can't remember.' Edge shrugged. A film of cold sweat had formed on his brow. 'It doesn't matter... Look, I aim to get a shave and a clean-up. All right with you?'

'Just watch how you go, mister. I can see there's no point in giving you advice.'

'No point in tramping around on my shadow either,' was Edge's dry rejoinder. He rose abruptly, crossed the room, and shouldered through to the street.

Moze Gall watched in a sort of daze as the swing doors flapped at the tall man's back. He rose, pulled his hat down on his forehead, and hurried after the stranger. 'John Tolliver?' he breathed in a strangled whisper. 'But who...'

He overtook Edge just as he reached the barber's shop. A sharp call brought the big fellow swinging around, right hand dropping to his side. 'Just a minute, mister.'

Edge waited until he drew level. He mustered a faint smile. 'What is it now, Sheriff? Am I doing something that displeases you?'

'Your name, mister ... I didn't hear your name.'

Edge's smile froze on his lips and his eyes appeared to ice over as well. Then he relaxed, his hesitation only momentary.

'Call me Worth,' he said. 'Anything else you want to know about me?'

'I'd just like to know how long you're going to last. Watch your step, mister.'

'That's the second time you've warned me, Sheriff, and if it makes you any happier I'll promise to do just that.'

Edge went on into the barber's shop and

Moze Gall stood there in the bright sun-light, swearing under his breath. It seemed that everything he said or did today was designed to boomerang on him.

He turned his head as Mark Caddon and some of his men, Gil Rimmel among them, emerged from Moon's saloon. They switched direction when they saw him and Gall met them halfway.

'You look all het up, Moze,' Rimmel declared with a sardonic twist at his lips. 'Don't he, Boss?'

'Mark, I've got something to tell you,' the sheriff said after stabbing a hard look at the foreman. 'That stranger... He gave me a nasty jolt back there in Foster's. Know what he said? Told me he'd heard that John Tolliver'd been shot to death at Crazy Woman Pass.'

Caddon rocked up on his heels. He pulled himself together quickly. 'But everybody knows Tolliver shot himself, Moze. Say, that happened all of ten, twelve years ago. How come this bird knew about Tolliver?'

'Said somebody told him a story. Queer, isn't it?'

'Queer,' Caddon echoed, worried in spite of his affected indifference. He glanced at his foreman. 'What do you make of it, Gil? Anything?'

'I guess it bears thinking about,' Rimmel decided with a frown gathering between his eyes. 'But you did say you figured he struck you as familiar, Boss.'

'He says his name's Worth,' Moze Gall enlarged. 'New handle to me.'

'Do you think he was telling the truth?' Caddon wondered.

'If you want to know what I really think, Mark, I'll tell you,' the lawman said in a rush. 'I reckon he knows more about this town and this territory than he lets on. He might be somebody we should know from away back.'

'Wait a minute!' Gil Rimmel exclaimed. 'Don't the name Tolliver mean more than a homesteader shooting himself? There was a kid, remember. Tolliver had a kid. Must have been about thirteen or fourteen at the time. Old Jim Brock took him in. Can't think of his name, though.'

'Edge,' Caddon said in a flash of recollection. His eyes gleamed with awakened memory, with something else, too, that he was quick to trap and hide. 'It's John Tolliver's brat come home to roost, by heaven!'

'And he figures that his old man didn't die accidentally.' Moze Gall said weightily. 'Mark, do you suppose–'

'I'm supposing nothing,' Caddon grated. 'Look, Moze, I don't care who this stranger is, or why he's in these parts. But I do know he's going to get his tail trimmed if he doesn't clear out. Is he still at Foster's place?'

'Gone to the barber's,' Gall explained. His face became pinched with anxiety. 'Mark, you're not going to start something right here in town?'

'You get back to your office,' Caddon told him. He might have been addressing a roustabout on his ranch. 'Just leave this to us.'

Moze Gall started to move away; he halted, annoyed and angry, tugged at his beard. 'I don't want any more shooting. It won't go down well. You'd better remember that, Mark.'

'I told you, Moze, leave it to us. Go sit in the sun for a while and quit worrying.'

When the sheriff had ambled off, Mark Caddon stared at his back for a moment, then turned to his man. His features were set in a determined mask. 'Gil, you come with me. You, too, Pritch. I reckon you've got a better reason than any of us for meeting John Tolliver's whelp.'

Pritch Stevens quailed briefly. He swallowed hard. 'You're breaking one of your own rules, Boss,' he complained. 'You said you'd never throw mud at a man. You promised you'd never mention that again.'

Caddon laughed and pushed his knuckles into Pritch's ribs. 'Just one of my little jokes. My humour's usually in bad taste... The rest of you fellas stay in the street,' he advised the others.

He gripped his horse's reins and turned towards the barber's shop. Gil Rimmel and Pritch Stevens followed at a distance, Rimmel combed the street with his eyes, squinting against the sunlight. There was no sign of Moze Gall now. Rimmel felt a certain sympathy for the lawman. He had always suspected that Caddon gave him a monthly pay-off, but he couldn't be sure of that.

They left their horses at the store flanking the red and white barber's pole and Caddon went over to peer inside. Edge Tolliver was still there.

Edge lay back in a chair with a large towel draped about his neck. His chin and jaw were covered with soap, and the barber was stropping his razor, chatting all the while.

'Yes, sir,' he was saying. 'A man in my position hears most of what's going on hereabouts. And I can tell you there's plenty happening about now. But a riding job...

Well, if I wanted a job chousing cattle I'd head out to Mark Caddon's spread. Finest ranch in the country, I'm told.'

'That's a mighty nice compliment, Jethro,' Caddon remarked from the doorway. 'No – don't get up, friend,' he added when Edge jerked on his chair. 'My, but you do look pretty with all that soap! Don't let it get into your eyes, though. Sure smells nice, as well...'

Edge's eyes, reflected in the mirror, were like chips of blue ice. He watched Pritch Stevens move over to the left of the room while Gil Rimmel stood at the doorway. The barber sucked in a breath. He tried to resume his customary blithe chattiness.

'Say, this is my busy day! You know, Mr Caddon, it's a funny thing, but when I start talking about somebody he usually pops up out of nowhere. Just like that!'

'Maybe you got some sort of magic touch, Jethro,' Caddon observed with a faint sneer. 'How about it?'

Jethro Pickens knew that something was amiss, something that had to do with the stranger sitting in the chair in front of the big mirror. He laughed nervously. 'Hey, what about that now! Maybe I ought to buy me one of those crystal balls, and–'

'Shut up, Jethro,' Caddon snapped. 'You're not nearly as entertaining as you believe you are.'

The barber reddened to the roots of his thinning hair. 'Yes, sir, Mr Caddon! What – what can I do for you men?'

Caddon pointed to a neighbouring empty chair in front of another large mirror. This one had a theatre poster with a scantily clad girl pasted on to the top left-hand corner. 'Sit down,' he invited Jethro. 'Give yourself a shave. Trim your nails or something.'

'But my customer...'

'Oh, him? We'll take over from here, friend. Close the door, Gil.'

The barber's nerve broke. He scurried for the door to try and slip past the Tumbling C foreman. Rimmel grabbed his shoulder and heaved him back inside. Jethro slumped down on the bench against the wall, his eyes oscillating wildly, his breathing shallow and noisy.

'Just sit tight or I'll give you a real close shave,' Rimmel threatened. He winked broadly at his boss, indicated Edge Tolliver who was still under the towel and who had not moved an inch. 'What say I finish shaving this bird? Give me a chance to keep my hand in.'

Caddon smiled briefly, sobered. He sank down on the chair beside Tolliver, plucked the towel free and flung it into his lap. 'Wipe your face.'

Edge cleaned some of the soap from his chin and mouth. If he was worried about the unorthodox visit he did not betray the fact. Caddon gripped the arm of the chair and swivelled it around until the younger man was facing him. The big head rolled a little as the examination continued, first to one side, then the other. Thick lips pouted.

'So you're this Mr Worth I've been hearing about? It's what you said your name was, friend, isn't it?'

'If Sheriff Gall told you something, then I reckon you can believe him,' Edge agreed coolly. 'He strikes me like a man of integrity.'

'All right then, Mr Worth...' Caddon brought a thick cigar from a vest pocket, bit the end off and spat the shreds at the cuspidor. He struck a match by digging a thumbnail into the sulphur. '...you can tell me in confidence if that really is your name. Or maybe you decided to tell the sheriff only half of it?'

The sudden widening of the tall man's eyes was the giveaway sign. Mark Caddon thought it amusing enough to warrant a hard, unpleasant laugh. He pointed a reprimanding finger.

'So you lied to the sheriff then? You gave him a false name? That usually means a man's got something to hide. In fact, Mr Worth, or whatever you call yourself, I happen to *know* that you've got something to hide.' Caddon lowered his tone, leaned forward so that his nose was almost touching Edge's. 'Your name's Tolliver, isn't it? Edge, or Edgeworth? You're John Tolliver's kid. You got a notion to come back to that old Eagle River country, the ranch at Spanish Ridge. Well, that's all right with me, mister. But I want to know why you came back to this neck of the woods. And before you tell me you returned to claim what's your own, let me tell you that you can't claim a damn thing. There's nothing out there for you, Tolliver, not now, not tomorrow. Not ever! Do you get all that?'

Edge finished wiping his face. He could see the barber again later. He tried to keep all three of them inside his range of vision.

'Seems to me you're forgetting something, Mr Caddon,' he said after a short pause. 'Dad never sold the Spanish Ridge ranch, so legally it's mine.'

'But the Wilsons are on it,' Caddon

pointed out. 'They moved in shortly after you disappeared. Jim Brock said your father left him the deeds of the place. Are you telling me that Brock's a liar and that the Wilsons are no better than squatters?'

Edge's instinctive reply died on his lips. So that was the story old Jim Brock had put around? It had been the old-timer's way of trying to keep the Tumbling C at bay.

'What about an answer,' Caddon pursued, taking a fierce puff on his cigar. 'Is Jim Brock a liar?'

Edge shook his head. 'Of course not.' A lot of thoughts were threshing around in his brain. That girl with the honey-gold hair ... the kid brother who had spoken out for Rufe Gates. Now old Jim Brock, Jim hoping that one day Edgeworth Tolliver might come back to Spanish Ridge, might he strong enough to stake a claim to what he believed was his own. Still ... if he rode out there and staked that claim, what would the Wilsons do – Barbie and the boy Vern – and whoever else might be living on the place?

'I don't think he's telling everything,' Gil Rimmel decided. Rimmel was beginning to feel uneasy. He didn't like the way they had burst in here and intimidated Jethro Pickens. One of these days the Tumbling C boss would push his luck too far.

'We'll see,' Caddon growled. 'We'll get to the bottom of it all right.'

'No matter how it goes, Mr Caddon,' Edge said, 'Spanish Ridge is no concern of yours. You don't own it and you never will. And now that I'm back...'

'Not for long, mister,' Caddon hissed. He switched his attention to the barber. 'Jethro, I'd say it's time you took a break and had a cup of coffee. Head along to the cafe, and don't be in a hurry getting back.'

The barber was in a torment of fear by then. His eyes locked with Edge's in the mirror. Edge managed a thin smile.

'Don't worry, pard. They're running what is known as a tall bluff. They can't touch me and they know it.'

Jethro started for the door and Gil Rimmel stood in his path. 'He might head straight for Moze's office, Boss.'

'No, he won't,' Caddon retorted. 'Jethro, you wouldn't like the name of sneak, would you?'

'No, sir, Mr Caddon. You know me. I might talk a lot in here, but I certainly don't spread rumours.'

'I had you figured, Jethro. Let him past, Gil.'

Rimmel stood aside to let the barber reach the street, and that was when Edge acted. He lunged from the chair and smashed his fist into Mark Caddon's mouth. The rancher yelled and made a grab for his revolver, but Edge Tolliver had not finished with him. His boot swung up and took Caddon in the stomach, throwing him against a shelf where razors and shaving mugs were arranged. The shelf cracked under the weight and toppled over, spilling everything to the floor.

Edge ducked as Pritch Stevens fired from the hip. The bullet smote a chair back and whined on to turn a mirror into flying shards. Then Edge had his own Colt free and the muzzle was spurting flame and smoke. Pritch Stevens yelled in agony and was flung into a mad spin.

Gil Rimmel held his fire, fearful of hitting Caddon or Stevens. It gave Edge the opportunity to crash into him, right elbow sawing for his chin. Rimmel managed to evade the blow, but reeled as Edge slashed the barrel of his gun against his nose.

By then Mark Caddon was on his knees, trying to claw his revolver free. Edge saw all this from the corner of his eye. He grabbed one of the chairs and flung it at the cowman, whirled to gain the back door of the shop.

Boots were pounding on the street boardwalk. Men were shouting at the top of their voices. Back of all the clamour, Edge fancied he heard Moze Gall bellowing orders.

He paid no heed, darted across the back lot. And, just as he thought he had a clear run along an alley, two men burst round a corner and began shooting into the air.

'Halt! Stand where you are, mister...'

Edge flung a couple of bullets in their general direction, crossed the lot and reached the alley. He broke off half way along and leaped a fence that put him into a small vegetable plot. He tripped over a barrel and hit the earth on his face. A fat, dark-featured woman with long hair tumbling around her shoulders screamed at him.

'Come back, you wrecker!'

Edge scrambled upright, vaulted the opposite fence. He was in another alley now, and he knew the livery stable was not far away. He must get to his horse and make a fast getaway. But if some of Caddon's crew were holed up at the livery he was done for.

FIVE

He halted when he reached the corner of the livery stable and glanced along the main street. Five or six men were milling around at the front of the barber's shop. There was no one heading this way. He went on into the stable.

'What's happening, mister?' the hostler asked him. 'Heard shooting down the road...'

'Looks like Mark Caddon's boys are getting in a bit of target practice.' He brushed past the man. 'I'm taking my horse.'

'I'll fetch your gear.'

Edge lost no time in saddling up. The stableman went outside to look along the street. When he returned he had a suspicious glint in his eye.

'You 'pear to be in a mighty big hurry, mister.'

'That so? Well, I got scared one time when a gun went off.' He tightened the girth, vaulted to the saddle. 'See you around, Dad.'

He angled away from the main street, found an alley that forked into the direction he wished to follow. When he reached the outskirts of Cedarville he viewed the sprawl of buildings behind him. No man-hunters on his trail. No sign of any of the Tumbling C bunch. In a way he was surprised at them allowing him to slip off like this. But the shooting at the barber's shop had caused a stir that would not be in the best interests of Mark Caddon or Sheriff Gall. The Tumbling C boss would prefer to deal with Edge Tolliver where there were no witnesses around.

Riding north and west, Edge wondered if Caddon would have gone as far as killing him at the barber's place. But there was no doubt that the message given John Tolliver's son was abundantly clear – he would be in mortal danger every hour he stayed on this range.

When he was about three miles out from Cedarville Edge glimpsed someone in the distance. His jawline lumped and his pulse-beat quickened with excitement. It looked as if Caddon had sent someone after him.

To make sure he was being trailed, he made a sharp swing into the east, skirting the shores of a lake and winding through a section of hilly country. At length he was facing a high, vaulted slash in a line of cliffs that provided access to a canyon. There was a natural rock stairway where he could let his horse climb to a wide spur that afforded an excellent vantage point. He reached the spur and reined down, patting the claybank's neck while he squinted into the distance. Yes, to be sure! The rider back yonder had made the deliberate switch necessary to come after him.

A grim smile puckered the corners of Edge's mouth as the claybank gingerly picked its way back to the canyon mouth. He dismounted and settled down among the massive boulders to wait. He smoked a cigarette while the sun slanted slowly into the west. These rocks radiated the heat they had collected during the day. Flies hummed and buzzed in persistent, irritating clouds. Away up yonder among the soaring escarpments three or four buzzards glided and circled. An eagle screeched peremptory warning to invaders.

He made several climbs on foot to make sure the man behind him was still bent on pursuit; he still was. He was steadily drawing closer, disappearing occasionally beyond a clump of rocks or brush, then coming into view once more. Edge saw him emerge from a thicket of oak and cedar but, instead of following the obvious tracks, he shifted abruptly towards the north.

Edge frowned, suspecting some new trick; this was the last thing he had expected to happen. He stayed under cover until he was certain that the horseman intended continuing in a northerly direction. What did it all mean – that the hunter had lost the trail? Extremely unlikely. That he was an innocent traveller, with no interest in the man who had come back to claim the Spanish Ridge layout?

By then Edge was more annoyed with himself than with that unknown rider. He allowed the man to cover a safe distance, then mounted the claybank and rode out of the rocks, settling on a course that roughly ran parallel with the trail the horseman in front of him was following. The sunset flares bathed the landscape in coloured streamers – crimson, yellow, saffron, with bands of steely grey widening and gradually predominating.

It was almost dusk when Edge caught sight of the traveller once more. By then they were high up in the north end of the range that flanked the boundaries of Tumbling C land and that owned by Gard Miller. It was becoming more evident that this trailing exercise was pointless. But his curiosity had been whetted and he might as well find out the identity of the man out there in the gathering darkness. Even if he broke off the chase at this juncture it would be full dark by the time he reached Spanish Ridge, so that switching direction, as he had done, now meant making a change to his plans. He would not approach the Wilson place until morning. It had taken him ten years to make his way back to this range and another day would make little difference.

He was leaving a stand of timber that gave on to a park of sorts when he saw the rider up ahead halt. Edge caught his breath when the man put his fingers to his mouth and emitted a thin whistle that rose to a piercing note. Now a second horseman materialised out of the gloom. The two of them came together, and Edge was able to hear the dim murmur of their voices. Soon there was another sound, the distant lowing and blatting of cattle on the move. Without further ado, the men in the gathering shadows crossed the park and were soon gone from sight.

Edge shook his head from side to side wonderingly. He cuffed his hat brim up from his brow, deciding to stay where he was for a couple of minutes. A scuffle on his right caused his hand to drop to his gun, but then he saw the outline of a deer briefly before it, too, vanished. He gripped the claybank's reins and angled towards the stretch of parkland.

He topped out a brush-fringed hummock and saw a valley of sorts falling away below him. Then he spotted the two riders and pulled back towards the brush screen. He watched the riders go down the valley slopes. There were other horsemen down there, and perhaps two hundred head of cattle. The animals were churning in on themselves, milling in confusion. Their plaintive lowing came to Edge's ears in a gusty clamour.

One of the men shouted and a leader was thrust out of the herd. Soon a trickle of dark hides followed the one being pushed. Some of the cattle tried to make a break, but they were quickly rounded in and pushed after the rest.

There was a film of sweat on Edge's brow now. The air pulsated with danger, with dark significance. A bystander had no business here, and there would be short shrift for a spy of any description. The man he had thought to be following him, and the others down there in that shadow-cloaked valley, were all involved in making a raid on Gard Miller's Triangle M stock.

The herd was swung around and pressed towards the outlet, which was off on Edge's right. The first of the animals were fast approaching the opening, the herders riding this way and that. Edge saw some other commotion further down the valley slope. The figure of a man whom he had not thought to be so close loomed up in front of him. There was a sharp cry, and then a six-gun belched flame and smoke. A bullet whined over Edge's left shoulder and slammed into the trees behind him.

Voices pealed back and forth as he grabbed his claybank and went into the saddle. Someone shouted: 'Hold on, there!'

Edge kept going, resisting the temptation to return another burst of gunfire. He jammed his heels into his horse's flanks and the beast surged into a crazy, headlong run that lacked rhythm and any sense of direc-tion. Gunfire was rattling viciously from two quarters now and he threw himself low in the saddle, at the same time grabbing his gun and snapping off a couple of shots.

The claybank hit the edge of the park once more and pounded across the clearing. Then it was bursting through a stretch of trees which, in turn, gave on to a slope that pitched much too sharply for Edge's liking. Expert horseman though he was, he had the utmost difficulty in staying in the saddle. His heart warmed to his mount's gameness and surefootedness. The sky was so dark by then that it was like floundering into a black, bottomless maw, with little hope of ever reaching the bottom.

The bottom was reached however, and Edge rode like a maniac for another ten minutes. When he hauled the horse in for a breather he found himself on the lip of yet another elevation, with the grass country tipping far below. He let the claybank take to the slope, but his heart was in his mouth until he had gained the flats where the air was laden with the smell of grass and sage.

He took a breather here, risked making a cigarette and flicking a match alight. He studied the black tumble of country above him with a morose slant to the corners of his mouth. Why hadn't things worked out as he had planned them? Where did he pick up the threads?

One thing seemed certain; the rustlers had decided it was more important to stick with the rustled cattle than to set about tracking the unknown rider who might have been spying on them.

He moved off at length, drifting towards the south and east, and soon seeing the first glimmerings of starlight in the vaulted heavens.

His thoughts reverted to that mysterious rider from Cedarville. If only he had stuck closer to the man he might have managed to establish his identity. That, in turn, might provide some clue about the whole of the owlhoot pack. It would have been something for Sheriff Gall to work on. Gall might not be so keen on going after the cattle-thieves; he might be content to get fatter and lazier. And there seemed little doubt that he was under Mark Caddon's thumb to a certain degree.

No, the best thing to do in the circumstances was to alert Gard Miller to what was going on. After all, it was Miller's stock that was being stolen, and if Miller's men could make an early start they might have a chance of overhauling the wideloopers.

So it was that Edge switched direction once again, making for the north-west. He might be a fool for putting himself to this bother, and he would gain small reward for his pains. These big cattlemen had always looked down their noses at the smaller outfits run by men like John Tolliver. Indeed, when Tolliver had been killed, few of them had disputed the accidental shooting theory or put themselves out by searching for the killer.

Nevertheless, he rode on towards Triangle M.

A dog barked as he hauled in on the front yard at the ranch headquarters. The alarm brought a figure hurrying out of the darkness from the direction of the bunkhouse. Then the front door was drawn open to emit a broad blade of yellow light.

'Who's there?' the man who emerged on the porch demanded.

'That Mr Miller? I've got news for you, sir. I'm sure a bunch of your beeves are being stolen at this minute.'

'What! Say, what the devil are you talking about? Are you drunk, man? Who are you?'

Edge was soon surrounded by a small group of men. Gard Miller hurried down the porch steps and pushed to the forefront. He peered up at the newcomer, trying to see his face.

'You're a stranger... What's this about my cattle being stolen?'

Edge lost no time in explaining about the

rider he had imagined was trailing him out of town. 'First off, I was dead sure he was following me, but then–'

'Say, Boss,' one of Miller's cowhands interrupted. 'It's the jasper who held Caddon at gun-point in Cedarville and made him take the rope off'n Rufe Gates' neck.'

'Is that so? All right, Burt, let him talk. But you'd better make it straight talk, mister.'

Edge grated his teeth, wishing now he had let the rustlers have their merry way. Still, the rancher's reaction might be understandable in the circumstances. 'While you're standing here gabbing, the thieves are getting further away,' he said coldly. 'But if that's the way you want it...'

'Where did all this happen?' Gard Miller queried, his manner changing.

Edge gave them directions relating to the ground he had covered. The hard ring to his voice convinced Miller that he was telling the truth.

'All right, boys,' he barked to his men. 'Saddle up and get out of here. You'll be moving faster than the cattle and there's the chance you might overtake them.'

'It must be that bunch we missed from the north end, Boss. Sure sounds like it.'

'Go fetch them, Luke.'

The cowhands scattered off towards the corral. Edge scrubbed the angle of his jaw, cleared his throat of dust and spat. He was pulling back to the gateway where the big Triangle M symbol hung when Miller raised a hand.

'Hold it, mister. I'd like you to hang on for a bit, if you don't mind.'

'Thanks all the same, Gard. But I'm heading some place else.'

'You're heading nowhere until I know something more about you, sonny,' was the cool rejoinder.

Edge couldn't be quite sure, but he believed Miller had his gun hanging by his side as he spoke. Edge swore.

'Sure is one hell of a country,' he lamented. 'Even when you try to help somebody you can be sure of only one thing in return – a good old kick in the teeth!'

'That all depends,' Miller said drily. He was a man of about fifty, lean and tough, moustached. He was just ever so slightly stooped at shoulder level. 'If it turns out I'm wrong I'll apologise. But you could be pulling a trick to clean this end of the range of men while your pards do their dirty work down here.'

'Of all the damn low-down notions! Mister,

I can see that the only way of making a go of the cattle business is to be as ornery as hell and as suspicious as a miser.'

The rancher's response was a hard chuckle. 'Get down and step inside,' he invited. 'You can see to your nag afterwards.'

He indicated that Edge should stay on the porch while he watched a group of his riders pelting off into the darkness. A lanky oldster with a rifle across his folded forearm appeared from the shadows and gestured for Edge to go on into the lighted hallway. Gard Miller followed him, saying to the old-timer: 'Can't say we haven't been expecting this, Mitch. Stay put out there for a piece, will you?'

'I'll be right here,' the other assured him in an easy drawl.

Edge was ushered into a large, well-appointed living-room. It reminded him of a magnificent ranch house he had seen in Texas where the architecture was ancient Spanish but all the furnishings were right out of a mail-order book. He was invited to take a comfortable, high-backed chair against the wall opposite the doorway. Gard Miller elbowed the door to and studied him for a few moments. The rancher's eyes were bright and alert. He had pouched his revolver, but his hand remained close to the walnut-stocked butt.

'You might put your shooting iron on the table there first,' he invited with a meagre smile.

'Now wait a minute, Mr Miller, you can't–'

'Want to bet? Do it, sonny.'

Edge did as he was told and resumed his seat. He produced the makings, lowered his head as he spilled some gold leaf into a corn-husk wrapper. Gard Miller drew up a chair, and when Edge appeared to be preoccupied with some vagrant thought he said sharply: 'Let's have it, mister. All you know about this business.'

'It isn't a whole lot. I told you how a man trailed me out of Cedarville. At least, I figured he was trailing me. But then he cut away from where I was at, and I decided to follow him.'

'What made you decide that? I can see you're a newcomer to these parts. Burt told me earlier about the man who'd broken up the hanging bee in town. So that was you?'

'Do you aim to hold that against me, too?'

'Never said I was holding anything against you.'

Edge remembered Gard Miller when he

had more meat on his bones and a lot more hair on his head. But he hadn't changed all that much. One thing was for sure, though: the rancher would not recall the Tolliver kid on Spanish Ridge.

'The nester was no rustler,' he told the rancher. 'A blind man could have seen he was innocent of the charge Caddon cooked up against him. Caddon just wants him out of the way, off his land. He was always like that. He's too old to change his habits much.'

'Always like that?' Miller echoed with quickening interest. 'How come you know all this about Mark Caddon?'

A faint smile relieved the set of Edge Tolliver's mouth. 'I know enough.'

'Look, mister, you'd better come right out with it. Your yarn about rustlers could be some kind of hoax. I've got patience, but not a whole lot of it. And I'd better tell you something else,' he added grimly. 'See Mitch out there with his rifle? You might not believe it, but he can get a squawk out of a dead cat if he puts his mind to it.'

Edge deliberated for the time it took to spin up another cigarette and light it. Then he said slowly: 'All right, Mr Miller, I'll squawk all I know. You remember John

81

Tolliver who used to run a shirt-tail outfit down at Spanish Ridge?'

Miller frowned, casting his mind back. 'Of course I remember Tolliver. But you're not–' He broke off and emitted a low whistle. 'But you are, by damn! I can see that you are. The kid. His name was...'

'Edgeworth,' his visitor supplied. 'All I ever got was Edge. I always hated that fancy name anyhow. I wondered what fool book my parents got it out of.'

'Edge Tolliver!' Gard Miller breathed. He stood up and extended his hand. 'Well, this sure takes some beating! But what are you doing back in these parts?'

Edge held the hand briefly. 'You might say I got an itch to head back thisaways, maybe have a look at the old place. I wanted to see how things were shaping up.'

'What about that now! Well, I'd better say straight off that I'm glad to see you again, son.'

'You really mean that, Mr Miller? The Cedarville fracas won't make you change your mind?'

'Of course it won't,' the other snorted. 'I always admired your dad. I was sorry about the way he was killed.' He noted the hard light that entered the younger man's eye.

'Sorry, Edge, I didn't mean to open old sores. But I always figured there was more to that shooting than ever came out.'

'You found it hard to believe Dad shot himself while he was cleaning his gun? Well, I never reckoned it happened the way they said. You see, Mr Miller, I'm certain that my father was murdered.'

Gard Miller's eye clouded. He bit his underlip. 'It's one thing saying it, son, and another thing proving it. There was never any proof one way or the other, you know.'

'You bet there wasn't! But what proof did Mark Caddon look for before he brought Rufe Gates to town and tried to hang him at the grain store?' Edge's voice rose. 'Gard, do you and the other ranchers on this range stand for that kind of play?'

Swift colour pushed through the cow-man's cheeks. 'There's things you don't understand...'

'Sure as hell's fire there is. But before I haul my freight out of this territory again I aim to understand plenty.'

Miller made no comment as Edge lifted his revolver from the table and slid it back in its pouch. He rose, straightened his hat.

'Edge, why don't you listen to reason? Let's talk this over.'

'Some other time, Gard.'

He passed the silent Mitch in the hall shadows and went on into the yard. Miller followed him to the porch and watched him lever himself into the claybank's saddle. He heard him muttering something to the animal. Then horse and rider were on the move and were soon swallowed in the darkness.

SIX

It was well past midnight when Edge hit the Eagle and followed the sullen flow of the river until he arrived at the off-shoot that was known as the North Fork. The moon was up and sailing on the torn rim of a ghostly cloud-pack. The air was tangy, spiced with sage. By daylight it would be rich with the fragrance of the wild flowers that festooned the moss-hung meadows.

Jim Brock's homestead was in darkness, the gaunt outlines of the buildings contriving a ragged rectangle of shadow in the surrounding gloom.

Now that he was here, Edge had qualms about disturbing Brock at this hour. The old fellow might be nervous, hair-triggered. He might shoot first if he saw someone on the prowl. A horse nickered in the corral at the back and the claybank replied in kind. Edge had reached the gate and was about to slide from his saddle when crisp warning rang out from the west corner of the house.

'You're far enough!'

A ripple of amusement caused Edge's mouth to crease in a smile. He was glad to be back here, visiting the old-timer who had taken him in on the death of his father.

'You wouldn't turn a tired and hungry man away, would you, mister?' he croaked with affected weariness.

'Want to bet two bits on that, mister?' Brock snorted. A rifle action clicked menacingly, then: 'If you don't hoof it right smart I'll put a bullet under your tail.'

Edge laughed outright. 'Golly, Jim, you're just as mean and sour-tempered as you ever were.'

'Hey, who are you? How do you know my name?'

'You can't guess? Well, let me put my nag up and we can talk about old times.'

He was able to see Brock now, a lean, gangling frame not unlike a scarecrow. The rifle was given a little wave and the homesteader ventured towards the gateway where the visitor sat.

'You've got a clear advantage, friend. I don't know you from Adam. But there's something about your voice all the same...'

'Figure you've heard it before some place, Jim?' Edge was enjoying himself now. The affection he had always felt for Brock was as strong as ever.

'Damn it, I have! No – stand there. Don't make a move. Range is boiling with sneaky characters that would plant a knife in your back as fast as say your name.'

'Range hasn't changed much, Jim, has it? Not in ten whole years. And I see Mark Caddon is as mean as ever. So is Pritch Stevens, and that cold-eyed Rimmel.'

'You know these parts terrible well, or else you're set on pulling a tall bluff on me, mister. But that voice – it keeps ringing in my head like some kind of bell.'

Edge dropped slowly to the ground, keeping his hands in view. 'Maybe I could jog your memory a piece, Jim. Think of a long-legged kid in cut-me-down pants. Think of him sitting at the old pot-bellied stove in there and asking you where you'd arrive at if you headed north instead of south.'

'Edge Tolliver!'

Edge was sure the old-timer would collapse in his excitement. He broke through the gate and flung his arms about Edge, then stood back to take in the height of the visitor and the breadth of his shoulders. He swore in wonderment, emotion making his voice quiver.

'I just can't believe it, boy. I can't believe it! So you've come back? I never thought I'd see you again. Not a man drifted out of the north or south but I asked about you. I kept on asking for years, I guess. I figured you might get around to writing some time. Then I thought you'd run wild and got yourself killed. Golly Moses! But come on inside, son, till I get a real look at you.'

Inside was much as Edge remembered it. But everything was on a smaller scale, as though a big sprawling place had somehow been reduced to doll's-house proportions. The horse-hide sofa remained in the corner to the right of the stove, where a couple of ancient, framed photographs hung on the wall. That was where he had lain awake nights, wondering how his father had come to be cleaning his gun and shot himself. The table, the stools, the stove that had kept a warm glow alive in the middle of winter – all had the power to resurrect memories that were mostly sad but which still retained traces of the sweetness that had come from friendship and understanding.

Brock soon had the stove stirred up, with a coffee pot dancing merrily on the heat. The light provided by the kerosene lamp anchored from the ceiling softened the spartan furnishings. Edge was prevailed on to relate as much as he could recall of his ten years of wandering. The water in the coffee pot boiled but was ignored. The oil ran low in the well of the lamp, but the fading of the light went unnoticed. Edge stopped speaking at last; Jim Brock let up with his eager questioning. The lamp was filled from a can; fresh coffee was brewed.

Edge ate venison and sourdough biscuits dipped in gravy. He sipped the glorious coffee and smoked, all the while watched by the soft, marvelling eyes of Brock.

'So you've been a trail-driver, miner, cowhand, and Texas Ranger...'

'And a heap of other things I'd be too ashamed to speak of, Jim.'

'Ahuh! But I reckon you never stooped to stealing or dealing off the bottom of the deck? Not that I'd blame you if you had.'

'Cold-decking and thievery are things I never thought I'd be much good at,' Edge told him with a grin.

'So back you come to the Eagle River country, and the first thing you do is manage to lock horns with Mark Caddon?' The old-timer laughed at that, but he soon sobered. 'Son, that won't do you any good at all. But finding that rustler nest... Well, you've done Gard Miller a good turn.'

'What kind of sheriff has Moze Gall turned out?'

'Some folks say one thing and others say something else.'

'I want to hear what you say, Jim.'

'He isn't such a bad sort,' Brock replied after brief thought. 'Say, did you intend taking over the old place? I let those kids squat on it.'

That brought the girl and her brother to mind again and Edge looked glum. 'Barbie Wilson has offered me a job, and I might take her up on it. The question about who owns what can come later. Barbie said riders are hard to find.'

'They are when they hear how they might have to tangle with Mark Caddon,' Brock agreed. 'But what's your reason for coming back if it isn't to move in on Spanish Ridge straight off?'

Edge looked at the homesteader straight in the eye as he confessed: 'To find out who killed my father. Can you think of a better reason, Jim?'

'No I guess I can't.' The older man poured more coffee, sighed. 'But facts are facts, son, and if Caddon has put the Indian sign on you for grabbing Rufe Gates from the grain-store scaffold, then you're really in for a hot time.'

It was late when they turned in, Edge refusing the bed that Brock offered. He would be quite happy to recall old times by sleeping on the couch once more.

'I guess I should apologise for running off the way I did,' he said. 'But if I'd told you what was in my mind you might have talked me out of it.'

'I'd have been against you leaving, sure, boy. But maybe it took all that to make you the man you are. I figure your dad would be proud of you right now.'

The night advanced, with Edge finding it hard to woo sleep. So many thoughts persisted in crowding his mind that he wondered if he would ever sleep again. The scene at the grain-store when he had treed Caddon's crew came back with vivid clarity. The fracas in the barber's shop had had a certain spice about it and would undoubtedly earn Mark Caddon's undying hatred. Next he reflected on the man he had imagined to be trailing him from Cedarville, his visit to Gard Miller's ranch, and so to Jim Brock's place where he could always feel at home.

He regretted nothing in spite of the

dangers that were piling up like walls of snow which must eventually become an avalanche. His spirits took a decided lift as he thought of the girl Barbie Wilson who had taken over the old Spanish Ridge ranch. He was looking forward to seeing her tomorrow – or should it be later in the day? – and asking her if she still needed a rider. Before he did that, however, he must tell her of his second run-in with Mark Caddon and warn her that, by hiring him, she would be leaving herself open to the wrath of Tumbling C.

He had barely drifted into sleep when something jarred him to wakefulness – the nervous whickering of a horse.

He sat up and strained his ears to pick up any strange sounds. Jim Brock was sound asleep in the bedroom, snoring gently. The sound came again, the horse nickering, the scuffle of hooves. It might be nothing more menacing than a coyote foraging for scraps, but again, it could be some of Caddon's crew, bent on wreaking vengeance. They might have watched him coming here. Caddon knew how Jim Brock had taken him in after the death of his father, and he might conclude that the homestead was the most likely place for the troubleshooter to hole up. Another possibility sprang to his mind.

The rustlers he had watched could have found out who he was and were anxious to keep him from talking.

Edge drew a slow breath, reaching for his boots. He was buckling his gun-belt about his waist when Jim Brock grunted, stirred, and then planted his gaunt shadow in the doorway.

'What's the matter, Edge? Say, you ain't drifting so soon?'

'Heard something outside, Jim. Somebody might be snooping around. Heard a horse fussing some. Listen –there it is again!'

Brock scratched his chest, yawned. 'If I jumped at everything I heard out there at night I'd be crazy by now. Maybe your nag's just tetchy. Some horses are worse than folks when they think they're being neglected.'

Edge was not so sure. He stood up and gave himself a shake down, slapped the gun at his hip. 'I'll sashay round the house to make sure.'

'Give me a minute and I'll go with you. You're liable to fall down the well in the dark.'

Brock was dressed in minutes. He lifted his rifle, worked the lever. 'I'll go out first,' he said. 'I'll mosey round back if you take the front. We'll meet over by the corral. You can cover most of the ground from there.'

Brock slipped into the shadows and Edge paused for a few seconds in the doorway. The moon had dropped behind silver-tipped clouds and the smell of rain was heavy in the air. The smell of rain always did something to Edge, resurrected jewel-drop, spring-day memories that belonged away back somewhere in early childhood. He could smell flowers in the rain, and wood-smoke, and there was always this pleasant murmur of friendly voices that made him feel secure.

He shrugged the sensation off while the corners of his mouth puckered into hard lines. Bringing his Colt to hand, he left the doorway and eased over to the front of the main building. He halted every few steps to listen and to probe the gloom.

The horse was whickering once more, and he guessed it was the claybank. Maybe old Clay didn't feel comfortable in that corral. He really was something of a temperamental cuss. When Edge reached the far corner of the house he halted with his shoulder against the wall, squinting through the thick shadows. He fancied he detected movement of some sort over yonder on his right. At the same time a challenge rose in his throat. But he choked it down in time. If Mark Caddon's men were on the prod for him they would start shooting on the instant he betrayed himself.

He moved on round to the gable and saw a gangling form drifting towards him like a wraith.

'That you, Jim?'

'It's me.' Brock was soon at his side, his narrow, long-jawed face held up like the edge of a spade. He reminded Edge of a hound trying to lift a scent. 'Don't see anything amiss,' he declared.

They stood for a while in silence, giving their senses free rein. Edge looked back to the spot where he had fancied something or someone had been lurking. A breeze hit his face now. A wind had sprung up and was soughing through the apple-trees that fringed the vegetable plot.

'You figure there's somebody here, don't you?' Brock whispered.

Edge gestured for him to be quiet. A scraping sound had reached his ears. It was followed by a clinking noise – the whirring of a spur rowel.

When the six-gun blasted he dashed his body against Brock, sending the old-timer tumbling to the ground. His own revolver barked twice, and it appeared to be the signal for a second ambusher to take chips in the game. This one was located out on the left, and not far from the corral.

Jim Brock had pulled himself together and was pumping off a couple of shots. He yelled warning as Edge darted off through the gloom, describing a weaving course so that he would make a poor target. A dark blob towered up in front of him and he triggered savagely, once, twice. He heard a hard cough, a groan. The form in front of him wavered, stumbled. The man was on his knees. Edge ducked as a crimson splash exploded in the darkness. A bullet whipped past his head. The gunman on his left sent three more shots at him, and Jim Brock's rifle boomed throatily several times.

The man he had thought to be finished was on his feet again. He raced towards a prancing horse, yelling at his friends as he went.

'Get out!'

Edge worked his trigger until the hammer fell on empty chambers. He reloaded frantically, hearing the whistling of a horse, the mad threshing of hooves. Boots hammered towards the corral and Brock's rifle cracked spitefully. Brock was attempting to keep the other bushwhacker pinned down, prevent him from escaping.

Edge saw him racing in pursuit of a figure. He called: 'Come back, Jim, you damn fool. Come back, I tell you!'

The homesteader paid no heed. Flashes of flame rent the darkness like lightning sulphur ripping holes in rain-laden clouds. Bullets peppered the clearing, whined and sang and ricochetted, and thunked into the walls of the house. The horses in the corral had begun a wild war-dance of their own, and Edge hoped the claybank would not leap the barrier fence. He was lurching in the wake of Jim Brock when he heard someone cry out. His heart skipped a beat as Jim Brock teetered like a drunken man before falling from view.

Powdersmoke stung Edge's nostrils. That was the raider over by the corral. Brock disposed of to his satisfaction, the would-be killer was concentrating on the upstart Edgeworth Tolliver.

He sent two rounds spearing the air around Edge, and before Edge could get a bead on him he had pulled himself aboard a lunging horse and was dashing off towards the trees. Edge's first impulse was to grab a horse from the corral and go after him, but then he heard Jim Brock calling something.

He found the old-timer and hunkered down at his side.

'You bad hurt, pard? Why in Sam Hill didn't you do what I told you?'

'I'm all right,' Brock grunted. 'Just a nick in the chest. Felt like I'd been hit by cannon shot. Look ... you go ahead and try and catch them before they escape.'

'Sure you're all right? Make it to the house?'

'Bet your life. Go do it, son. But watch they don't try some sidewinder trick.'

Edge scrambled his way to the lean-to shed and hauled out his saddle. He whistled for the claybank and the big horse came to the gate at once, trumpeting defiance at some unseen enemy. Edge lost no time in setting the rig and springing to the saddle. He left the homestead at a hard gallop in a wide, questing circle. He soon caught the pounding of hooves away out in front, but after a mile or so it was patent that the raiders were equipped with fresh horses and had a quick getaway route planned beforehand.

Even so, he stuck to the trail for thirty minutes or so, the fire of battle dying in his bloodstream to allow a slow fury that was partly frustration take over. The rain started falling as he finally renounced his bid to overtake the raiders and angled back towards Brock's homestead site. The deluge hit him long before the outlines of the buildings materialised out of the murk.

He expected to be challenged by Brock as he crossed the yard, and frowned worriedly when he heard nothing but the forlorn dripping of rain-water from the eaves. He went on to the barn and stripped his horse. He rubbed it off quickly and roughly, then turned it into a stall. Perhaps Jim's wound had been more serious than he had known or admitted. He ducked through the rain until he reached the spot where he had left Brock, but there was no one there.

'Must have made it inside,' he muttered. 'Wonder does the old coot drink the way he used to...'

He was surprised to find the front door open but no lamp-light in evidence, and, as if to accentuate the feeling of dread that was creeping over him like a chill wind from the mountains, the rain dripped incessantly. The wind rose and scoured a path around the building. It shrilled and keened, evoking the recent turmoil comprised of barking guns and choking cordite.

Edge faced the dark maw of the living-room. 'Jim, are you there? It's me back again...' And when the hammering rain continued to mock him: 'Are you hurt, old-timer? Just make a noise so I'll know where you are.'

His fingers were unsteady as he fumbled for his tin matchbox, selected a lucifer and nailed into the fat lump of sulphur at the end. The light sprang up, flared, spread like yellow oil being poured over a dark surface. He pushed a chair to one side and went around the table to look at the sofa before going on to the bedroom. He had to strike another match to get a proper look.

It seemed as if Jim Brock actually did have the sofa in mind when he dragged himself into the house and across the floor. There were bloody streaks here and there. However, the old-timer had not been able to make it. He just hung there, one arm resting on the side of the couch, one leg stuck out at an awkward angle. His mouth hung open and his eyes stared back at Edge. It looked as if he had been trying to say something just before he died.

SEVEN

A muddy dawn was stirring in the east when Edge tamped the final spadeful of earth in place and gazed morosely at the mound where his old friend lay. Another wanton killing, he reflected bleakly, another crime to be laid at the door of Mark Caddon.

Edge had no doubt that the night riders had come from Tumbling C. They had concluded he would be visiting Jim Brock with the idea, perhaps of staying at the homestead for a few days until he got his bearings. They had come with the intention of putting Tolliver out of action before he had time to perpetrate any more mischief. Had Jim Brock stood in their way in any manner he would have shared the same fate. They would likely have killed old Jim in any case, to make sure he kept his mouth shut.

The rain had thinned out an hour ago and the swollen, grey-bellied clouds were fleeing towards the south. A weariness lay on Edge now, a sense of deflation and depletion. He put the pick and shovel back in the lean-to and washed up at the stand beside the door. He brewed a pot of coffee, then took the claybank out and rode for an hour, circling the area, thinking that some of Caddon's men might still be hanging around.

Back in the house, he fed some billets into the stove and put the kettle back on to heat, adding water and a couple of spoonfuls of the coarsely ground coffee. He smoked in the doorway while the sun burst out of the east with promise that would never be kept now. Had he looked some way other than at Brock's homestead, Jim would still be alive.

A milk cow lowed in the pasture behind the house. Birds began chirruping in the grove of trees. On a morning like this a man should have hope in his heart and be able to respond to the blandishments of a new day. But it was not to be so. The raiders had done for old Jim. It meant he had another reason for cutting out the rot that plagued this Eagle River country like a festering sore.

He added some grey sugar to the coffee and drank several cups. He stood there with his shoulder against the doorjamb and let his gaze roam speculatively where it might. Soon he would have to address the practicalities of the moment. Sheriff Moze Gall would have to be informed, of course. Not that Gall would bother to do much about the raid and the killing, he suspected. And if Edge showed his face in Cedarville for any reason, Gall might decide to lock him up, using the barber-shop fracas as an excuse for caging the nuisance.

He was heading for the barn to see to the claybank when he heard a rumble of hoof-beats cutting in from the north. He took his rifle and placed himself at the barn entrance. If this turned out to be more of Caddon's riders on another devil's spree he would give them a hot reception.

Soon he was able to see two horsemen come around the massive bulge lying at the foot of Eagle Butte. They came on steadily, but without haste, and when they were a little closer he was able to recognize the lean form of Gard Miller, bowed over his saddle-horn in that queer way he had of riding. Miller must have deduced, also, that Tolliver would spend the night with his old friend. Gard's companion was Fred Gipson, Miller's foreman. Gipson was a well set-up man in his mid-forties, weathered, sober of disposition, and characterised mostly by his taciturn nature.

Edge met the pair as they cleared the fence and pressed into the front yard. He had left his rifle in the barn but his six-shooter was hanging where it would be handy.

'Well, howdy, Edge,' Miller greeted. 'I wondered if I might find you staying with Jim. Frank here allowed you might go to Spanish Ridge.'

'Hello Frank. Glad to see both of you, Gard.'

Gipson fixed him with his slit-eyed, penetrating regard. 'Glad to see you again, Edge. I just about recall you. But I wouldn't have known you if I'd met you anywhere.'

They came out of their saddles, Miller sensing at once that something was wrong. Edge gestured wordlessly and the cowman paced away to where part of the tamped mound was visible. Gipson was dividing his attention between his boss and Tolliver. Gard Miller came back, eyes flashing in a face gone grey.

'Edge, what in hell happened?'

'It's Jim, sure enough, Gard. I woke up in the middle of the night when I heard a horse making a fuss. We were hunting around for prowlers when they started shooting.'

'How many?'

'Two, at least. Jim and me put them to running, but Jim wanted to grab one of them and was gunned down. I might have wounded one of them, but I can't be sure.'

The seconds dragged while Miller and his foreman stared at him. It was evident that Miller was badly shaken. 'Do you know who they were and why they sneaked out in the dark?'

'You should know the answers without asking,' Edge responded tautly. 'Mark Caddon's crew, for sure. They wanted to teach me a lesson.'

'But you can't prove it,' Gipson reminded him.

'No, I can't. But I won't quit till I find the killers and give them a dose of their own medicine.'

'Yeah, I guess I know how you feel,' Miller's foreman murmured. 'I reckon I'd feel the same way myself. But don't depend on Moze Gall in Cedarville, mister. He figures Caddon can do no wrong.'

'It's something I know already, Frank.'

'Look,' Gard Miller butted in, 'why not come home with us? We'll give you a steady job. If you persist in making war with Caddon there's only one way it can end.'

Edge was touched by the offer. Nevertheless he shook his head. 'Thanks, Gard, no. Did your men have any luck last night when they went after the rustlers?'

'That's really what brought us over here,' Miller explained. 'The boys overtook them up in the hills. There was a lot of shooting and the cattle spooked. But we saved more than half of the bunch and I hope they'll all be rounded up eventually.'

'And the owlhooters?'

'Oh, they scattered to hell and yonder.'

'You've no idea who they are? No names? Nobody you can get your hands on and squeeze some information out of?'

'I've a notion,' Miller confessed with a hard smile. 'But one of these days I hope to get real proof. And when I do–'

'Caddon again?' Edge suggested.

Miller looked at his foreman before answering. 'That could be a dangerous thing to say, son.'

'Well, Rufe Gates wasn't so close-mouthed about it when they had his neck in that noose in town. Caddon must have seen Gates as a big fly in the ointment. But when will somebody find the guts to go after Tumbling C, Gard?'

Frank Gipson emitted a sour chuckle and spat between his horse's ears. 'You aiming to do that?' he prodded with grim amusement.

'I might try it.'

'Then good luck to you, Edge. And if

things get too sweaty you know where you can count on some friends. That right, Boss?'

'That goes for me, of course, Fred. Don't forget what I said about staying with us for a while.'

'Thanks, Mr Miller.'

Edge was lighter of heart as he watched the men ride back the way they had come. He stood with the sunlight growing warm and bright about him, the heat sucking up the moisture of last night's rain. Jim Brock had no relatives that Edge had ever heard of. His passing would mean little to anybody but himself and men like Gard Miller, men who would welcome the opportunity to make a solid strike against Tumbling C, but who were too tolerant – or perhaps too fearful of risking the combined wrath of Caddon and Moze Gall in Cedarville.

Edge took his claybank out and drifted south and east, travelling through the growing heat of the morning until he was skirting the homestead owned by Rufe Gates. Then he climbed on over Spanish Ridge, noting how the grass here was so green and lush. When he saw small clusters of grazing cattle his heart gave a leap and he realized just how much the killers of his father had taken from his life.

A tightness rose in his throat when he came within view of the buildings erected by his father and a few helpful neighbours, and even as he dallied with a faraway look in his eyes he saw a girl emerge from the house and go round to the corral where six or seven head of saddle-stock romped. He wondered if Barbie Wilson had learnt the identity of the stranger who had taken her neighbour's part in town yesterday. Would she really expect him to take up her invitation in relation to a job, or was that just so much friendly hot air?

Even if she was sincere about her offer, when she heard of his second run-in with Mark Caddon and of the raid at Jim Brock's place last night, she would drop him like a hot coal.

He moved on from Spanish Ridge without showing himself, much less announcing himself. He veered south until he hit the trail leading to Cedarville, and reached the town with the midday sun pouring down its relentless heat. There was no sign of the deluge that had recently swept the country. The main street had dried out into ridges of baked dust that gave easily before the claybank's hooves.

Making his way to the building housing the law office, Edge became aware of many eyes picking him out and following him. He knew that, here and there, small knots of people were gathering to whisper and to speculate in connection with what fresh trouble this nervy stranger might stir up before he left.

He brought his mount in to the sidewalk, and was looping the reins to a post when someone spoke. 'Howdy, young Tolliver! Going to give old Moze another run for his money?'

The speaker turned out to be a loafer who was sprawled on a nearby bench, hat tilted over his forehead. Bright eyes twinkled mischievously, and Edge felt a little thrill at the use of his name. He nodded acknowledgement, and was moving on to the law office when the loafer spoke again.

'Better watch out, mister,' he said in a lower key. 'That hell-raising you started yesterday has got folks talking. A lot of people are feeling low because they stood back when Caddon tried to hang the nester.'

'That's their affair.'

Edge knuckle-rapped the open door of the sheriff's office and heard a chair leg scraping. Moze Gall's voice sang out: 'Come on in.'

He was seated behind his desk, and had evidently been brooding on something. At sight of Edge Tolliver his mouth went slack and his right hand wormed its way to the revolver at his side.

'Get the hell out of here,' he breathed thinly.

'Take it easy, Sheriff...'

'Easy! After all the mud you've stirred? After starting a fight along in Jethro Pickens' shop. And you nicked Pritch Stevens... Mister, I've got enough on you to keep you behind bars for a couple of years.'

Gall struggled on to his feet, brought his gun into view and levelled it.

'Put that damn thing down,' Edge choked.

'Take me for a fool, don't you? You made me look smaller'n a rabbit yesterday. You could have started a riot in town.' Moze Gall was sweating. His lips peeled away from his teeth. 'I've a good mind to shoot you down where you stand. How about that? That would put an end to your hell-raising for good, and no mistake!'

'Maybe so,' Edge said from tight lips. 'But what do you tell folks after you shoot me and I'm lying here dead? Can't you guess what they'll say, Sheriff, especially as they'll see I never got a chance to defend myself?

Even Caddon will have a job squaring that for you.'

'I don't need Caddon, you bastard.'

'Why don't you tell him that? Why can't you be your own man?'

'Curse you, I am my own man.'

'All right. Go ahead and cuss me out. Why not? Shoot me if you can't bear to have me haunting your dreams at night. Giving a man a chance is hardly your style, is it? How much does Caddon pay you for turning a blind eye to his scheming?'

Gall's eyes glittered balefully. The sweat beaded and trickled down the planes of his face. There was an ominous click as he cocked his revolver.

'What's holding you, Moze?' Edge whispered huskily. 'All you have to do is squeeze the trigger. But I'll not be going out on my own, mister. I'm fast and I'm accurate, and I'll manage to plug a couple of holes in your miserable hide before I cash.'

Edge thought he had pushed him too far. His own heart was thumping so violently he was certain the sheriff must hear it. Gall tugged at his collar and Edge found himself staring at the mole on his cheek. Old memories surfaced once again, turgid, rank with bitterness.

The lawman surprised him by croaking: 'What do – you – want me to do?'

Edge released a hard breath. 'All I want you to do right now is put that iron away and get back into your chair before somebody comes in. You wouldn't want that?'

The bearded man moved almost blindly. The gun hand wavered, fell. He restored the weapon to its pouch with a little vicious push, slid down on to the chair and wiped his brow with a polka-dot kerchief.

'You'd better make some sense from now on, Tolliver. You're labouring under the delusion that your father was murdered. All the evidence of an accident was there.'

'Of course it was. Planted by the killers!' Edge perched on the desk. 'Now, get a couple of things straight, Sheriff. Caddon started all that trouble at the barber's. Jethro can tell you the truth if he's not too scared. And last night I trailed a certain party who turned out to be a rustler. I saw him meet his pards with a herd that belonged to Gard Miller. They caught on I was watching and started shooting.'

'More trouble! You're crazy, mister. You're away out of your depth.'

'Maybe. But I can swim pretty good. Anyhow, I told Miller what I'd seen and he sent his boys after the cattle. He managed to recover some, but the owlhooters got clear. Now I'm getting to the part that matters, Sheriff. I spent what was left of the night at Jim Brock's place up by Eagle Butte. We had visitors in the middle of the night. They turned their guns on us and Jim was shot.'

'Jim Brock killed!'

'I buried him this morning. I don't know who the raiders were, but I've got a fair idea. Maybe you have, too. I'm telling you all this in case Caddon gives you a different story. But I bet he's too wily to let on he knows anything about that raid.'

'If what you say is true I'll look into it,' the lawman said raggedly.

A grim little smile tugged at Edge's mouth. He believed he had Moze Gall on the run, and he might as well take full advantage of the fact. 'You'd better do that, Sheriff,' he said bleakly. 'You damn-well just better. If you don't find old Jim's killers I'll have to find them for you. And I won't be bringing them back alive.'

Gall tried to say something else, but words failed to come. He looked grey and whipped. Edge was not fooled by this reaction. The sheriff would sit and brood; he would plan. He might even take Mark Caddon into his confidence, with the aim of getting Tolliver out of his hair for good.

Edge backed to the open doorway and slipped into the street. A group of curiosity-seekers hung around, but he paid no heed. He walked on to Foster's saloon where he drank a beer. Afterwards, he rode out of town, aware of the many eyes that followed him and mindful of the hatred that was probably festering in Moze Gall's belly like a dark poison.

EIGHT

His journey back into the north would have seemed almost a leisurely affair to an onlooker. But he took care to avoid the main trails where he might run into any of the Tumbling C crew. He was pleased with his trip to Cedarville and with the way he had handled Moze Gall. The sooner the sheriff realized he could not labour under Mark Caddon's shadow and pack a law badge at the same time, the better it would be for everyone.

Edge reached the Little Eagle, a tributary of the mother river, where there was a pool tucked into a bend flanked by a fringe of willows. This, in turn, was lorded over by cottonwoods. The inviting prospect proved too much for him. He off-saddled and picketed the claybank, then stripped and plunged into the water. He swam around for ten minutes or so, resisting the main current of the river, before returning to the grassy bank.

He was about to crawl out when he

realized that something was wrong. Back in the clearing where he had shed his clothing he noticed two horsemen watching him with sly amusement. Pritch Stevens was one of them and the other was a muscular, dark-browed bruiser whom Edge had never seen before.

'Ain't he a pretty sight, Lem?' Stevens drawled. 'And a man would think he had more sense than to go swimming without his shooting iron.'

'You mean this shooting iron here, Pritch?' The big fellow held Edge's gun aloft, en-joying its owner's discomfiture immensely.

'That's it, sure enough, Lem. Throw it over yonder in the brush. But make sure you take the shells out first.'

Edge swept the wet hair from his eyes. He cursed himself for a careless fool. After being so cautious on the trail he had behaved like an idiot when he arrived at the river! It was possible that Stevens and his sidekick had trailed him from town, or perhaps they had simply stumbled on him here. In any case, they could scarcely contain their glee over their stroke of good fortune.

Edge fought the quick terror that entered his stomach and coiled. The walls of his throat were so tight he could scarcely breathe. He stood there, knee-deep in the water, wondering what the outcome would be. For the second time in his life he felt utterly defenceless and totally vulnerable.

'What's the big idea, Stevens?' he growled. 'You want something?'

'What gave you that notion, Tolliver? I don't want a thing from you. But Lem Slater here was hoping to make your acquaintance. That's so, Lem, ain't it?'

'You just said it, Pritch. Hear this gent is behaving something awful since he hit these parts. Getting into Mr Caddon's hair. Carrying sneaky stories to the law in Cedarville. Shooting at you...'

'Makes him look quite a big fella, Lem, don't it now?'

'Sure as hell does,' Slater nodded. 'But I like them kind of big, pard. Tangling with big gents makes life taste real sweet.'

Stevens gestured for Edge to come on out of the river. 'Get into your rags, boy,' he grated. 'And make it quick.'

Edge bit back a retort and went to his clothes. They watched in silence as he drew each item on over his wet body. He pushed his feet into his boots and rose to face the pair squarely.

'So you're going to shoot me down the

way you shot Jim Brock? The way you murdered my father...'

Stevens drew a ragged breath. His eyes snapped under some shock, and Edge knew that fate was being kind to him at last. That flickering of dark guilt convinced him that here was one of the men who had been involved in the murder of his father over at Crazy Woman Pass. The revelation sent a queer, heady thrill running through him. But what could he do about it? He was at the mercy of these men; he might not even be alive five minutes from now.

'What are you talking about?' Stevens demanded. 'What happened to Brock?'

'You know fine what happened to him. Likely it was your bullet that put him down. And what about my father?'

'What's he going on about, Pritch?' Slater wanted to know.

Sweat glistened on Pritch Stevens' brow. 'He's just talking, Lem. Way I see it, he needs his mouth buttoned up for a spell.'

Stevens produced a quirt and, before the true nature of his intentions dawned on Edge, the thong was curling and cracking and raking his face and neck. The sharp, agonising pain acted like a goad on him and he sprang at the thin man, taking another cut from the quirt before managing to fasten his fingers on Stevens' sleeve and heave him from his lunging horse.

'Get him, Lem!' Pritch screamed.

Slater dropped to the ground and pushed his horse aside. He was as tall as Edge, wider in the shoulders, with long, muscular arms that ran out to huge, paw-like hands. Edge managed to evade the first vicious blow that was launched at him. But the momentum took him off balance and threw him to his knees. Before he could rise Stevens was at him again with the quirt, emphasising each stroke with a hearty curse.

'I'm going to gun him,' Slater warned his friend. 'Stand back...'

'No, damn you, Lem. The boss said–'

Tolliver's balled fist slammed into the lean man's stomach with the force of a loco-motive piston. Stevens buckled and went over, and Edge snatched at the quirt. He brought the loaded handle cracking against Pritch's skull and Stevens reeled, yelling in pain.

'Get him, Lem!'

The big fellow was already moving in with deadly intent. He felled Edge with a mighty blow to the temple that flattened him and bemused him momentarily. Edge saw the boot swinging at his face and went into a roll that took him into a patch of brush. The horses whistled and stamped. Edge came up with a thousand lights bursting in his brain. He knew that Lem's fist was mauling him, but there was simply nothing he could do about it.

Next, he saw Pritch Stevens on his feet, quirt at the ready, his face a mask of maniacal fury. He stalked Edge like a cougar. Edge went down before a brutal onslaught. He grabbed for Lem Slater's boot as it was stabbing in at his ribs, heaved and twisted, and flung the stumbling Slater into his companion.

Edge was making a dash to the spot where his gun-belt had been thrown when Lem reached him. He steadied and managed to break through the big fellow's guard. But Stevens was busy with his quirt again, swearing and lashing out like a madman. Agony piled on agony for Edge. He was moving instinctively at this juncture, more dead than alive. If only his limbs would heed the messages from his brain…

Voices reached him from a great distance. Someone was swearing hoarsely, groaning. It was a surprise to find that he was making the noise himself. A wave of sickness engulfed him, then he was back in the water, going under, but being partly revived by the coolness. Still, he was sinking, drowning. So this was the way he was to cash his chips, and there wasn't a solitary damn thing he could do about it?

High-pitched, mocking laughter reached his fuddled brain, succeeded in triggering a fresh burst of fury. He spewed water and coughed, but when he tried to strike out his arms had lost their strength. Fresh terror assailed him. His fingers touched something and he grabbed blindly, feeling a trailing willow branch. He held on, but the slender limb slipped through his fingers.

Then his feet touched sand and shifting gravel. He clawed again, caught the branch, and this time he managed to maintain the hold. He gulped air hungrily, clawed his way to the river bank and let himself go. After a while he tried inching himself up the bank to the grass, where he collapsed with exhaustion.

Minutes went by – it could have been hours – before his brain cleared sufficiently to allow him to think of his plight, to try and reason things out. Stevens and the bruiser called Lem Slater – were they standing above him, gloating, giving him time to recover so that they could resume their punishment?

After a while he turned on to his back, giving his face up to the heat. The purl and swirl and tug of the river current was like thunder in his ears. Over yonder somewhere a horse was shifting around. Could it be the claybank? But where were the Caddon men?

They had gone, he discovered eventually. They had left him to the mercies of the river, hoping it would finish their work for them. His flesh stung and recoiled where Pritch Stevens had lashed him with his quirt. The drops of water that trickled from his face were stained with blood. But at least he was alive, and yonder was Clay. And he knew beyond any shadow of doubt that the Caddon riders had not intended to kill him or have him drown. That was not in the rules that Mark Caddon had given them. Caddon had ordered them to rough him up but to stop short of killing him.

At length Edge made it to his feet, staggering like a Saturday night drunk. He reached the trees and leaned against a bole, getting more water up, fighting the overpowering nausea. The claybank sensed his plight and came over to nuzzle him. He fumbled at his belt, knowing there was something important he must attend to. His revolver and shell-belt. Had they taken his gun gear? No, Lem had thrown it into the brush over there.

He found the revolver and held the butt as he might grab the hand of an old and trusted friend. He slid bullets from his belt and loaded the chambers, then buckled the belt about his waist and snugged the Colt .45 home. He decided that, come what may, the next time he laid eyes on Pritch Stevens or Lem Slater he would give them a gutful of lead. When you got mixed up with men of their ilk you had to use the language they knew best.

Edge freed the picket rope and heaved himself into the saddle. His brain spun in feverish circles and he was slow in settling on the direction he needed to travel. He would bypass Spanish Ridge again, he decided. That girl and her brother must not see him in this state. Going to work for Barbie Wilson now would be out of the question. While he stayed on this range he would draw Tumbling C trouble faster than a magnet could pick up a nail.

He gigged the horse into motion, each movement awakening a dozen sores and bruises. Blood still dribbled from his left cheek and salted his lips, and he patted the weals gingerly.

A dozen times he was obliged to halt the claybank so that he might shake the muzziness from his brain and make certain he wasn't straying on to Caddon territory. He suspected every rock he passed of concealing a Tumbling C rider, that behind every bush a gun was ready and waiting to blast him into eternity.

He was on the slopes of Spanish Ridge before he realized it, and now he must veer sharply to the west. But where was he making for – Rufe Gates' place in order to cash in on the gratitude and sympathy of the man he had rescued from Caddon's hangrope? That had not been in his mind either. And then it came to him: he wished to return to Jim Brock's homestead by Eagle Butte. It was unlikely that anyone would ride along there for a day or so, which would give him time to lick his wounds and find his feet again.

He pulled his horse from the trail and climbed a sweeping rise where grass and wild flowers rose belly-high to the claybank. Flies hovered in clouds in the yellow heat; bees hummed lazily. He heard a cow lowing somewhere and it brought the rustlers to his thoughts, together with Rufe Gates' strong hint about Mark Caddon. It would be a nice note if the owner of the Tumbling C and Moze Gall in Cedarville were running a dirty game between them. Didn't the sheriff stick up for Caddon at every turn, shielding him from real justice? And if that was the true state of affairs then what would be so surprising about Gall drawing a renegade's pay?

A shout sent fear streaking along his backbone. His hand sought the gun at his hip and he endeavoured to straighten his body sufficiently to enable him to scan the surrounding terrain. His sight seemed weak and blurred, but he was sure there was a horseman down the slope on his left.

The cry came again, a ring of challenge in it. Edge dragged the claybank to a halt and waited. In his present condition it was impossible for him to make a run for it. If this was another representative of Caddon's crew, bent on giving him a rough time, he would greet the man with a belching six-shooter.

'Hey, mister, are you hurt?'

A boy's voice, he was sure, curious, refreshingly devoid of malice. He heard hoofbeats bearing in to where he waited, watched as a tow-headed youngster galloped into clearer view and hauled up to regard him intently.

'Hello, kid...'

'You're – the – the man that saved Rufe Gates from being hung. You're Edge Tolliver, aren't you? You sick or something, Mr Tolliver?'

Without waiting for an answer, the boy whirled his mount around and galloped off again. Scared, Edge thought with a touch of bitterness, just like the rest of the folks on this range. Still, he was only a kid. At that age Edge Tolliver had been a pretty frightened youngster himself. Many times he had known the cold clawing of fear at his vitals as he stood beside his father and faced Mark Caddon's riders.

If only he could make it to Jim Brock's homestead...

He was on the move again when the earth appeared to vibrate under the stamping of more hooves. He squinted against the sunlight and chuckled when he realized that the boy was coming back, and now he had someone with him – his sister, without doubt.

The thought of Barbie Wilson seeing him like this filled him with a queer, illogical dread, and he reacted accordingly – jabbing his heels at the claybank's flanks in an effort to get clear.

'Mr Tolliver! Please wait...'

They raced up quickly and the girl came out of the saddle in a lithe, reckless leap. The boy followed suit and gripped the claybank's bridle. Edge had a vision of a pretty face wreathed in concern, of a mass of wind-blown golden hair, and of red lips parted over small white teeth.

'Oh, Mr Tolliver, you're hurt!' she cried. 'What happened? Someone attacked you, didn't they?'

'Caddon's skunks, Sis,' the youngster gritted. 'They've been after him for helping Rufe in town. Isn't that so, Mr Tolliver?'

'I'm – all – right,' Edge muttered. 'Don't worry. I just took a – uh – toss in the stream.'

'You've been beaten,' the girl insisted. 'You're all torn and bloody. You must come back to the ranch and let me look at you.'

Edge protested, but he was too weak to argue and soon ran out of steam, so that he became amenable to the girl's demands.

With Edge holding on to the saddle-horn, the boy led the claybank out in front. Barbie followed at a short distance, glancing this way and that, her blue eyes sober, reflective. And once she stretched her fingers to the stock of the Winchester rifle tucked under her saddle fender, as though wishing to assure herself that she was prepared for any eventuality.

They reached the front yard without incident, and even at this juncture Edge started to explain that he was capable of looking after himself. But he never finished the sentence. He began sliding from his saddle to the ground, quite unexpectedly, and had slithered on down, senseless, before the girl or her brother could reach him.

NINE

When Edge opened his eyes he knew it was morning. The warm sun streamed through the window of the room where he lay. It turned out he was in bed, between sheets he had never known could be so clean and crisp and sweet-smelling. A breeze from the open window touched his face, teasing him with its promise of open spaces and freedom of movement. His eyes presently took in the room itself, settled on a jar with wild flowers in it, the blue of verbena, the bright flame of Indian paint brush. His gaze continued to roam this small space that was in one way familiar to him; in another, new and strange, evincing the sure, confident evidence of a woman's hand.

A door opened and the boy stuck his head through. His hair still stuck up like corn stalks, his freckled cheeks spread in a grin while his eyes danced merrily. There was an air of diffidence about him just then.

'Morning, Mr Tolliver. Feeling better?'

'Sure, kid. I'm feeling fine. You're Vern. I

129

heard your sister call you in town.'

'That's right. She's Barbie. And you're Edge Tolliver. You used to live here a long time ago. Rufe Gates found out all about you. Rufe said you'll never be without a friend while he can stand on his two legs.'

The terminology caused Edge to smile. 'That's sure nice to know. And speaking of standing on two legs, I suppose I'd better find out if I can stand on mine.'

'Don't try it, Edge!' the boy warned as Tolliver flung the sheets back and swung himself out to reach the floor. He saw that he was clad in a long night-shirt, a garment that had likely belonged to the youngster's father. He had no recollection of getting into it.

The girl's voice came through the open door and Edge hastily drew the bed-clothes back in place. Vern laughed at his antics.

'It's all right, Barbie. Edge is awake and getting out of bed.'

'What! You mean you allowed him...' She was in the room now, hair brushed back, aproned waist trim and attractive. 'Really, Mr Tolliver, you'll have to take it easy for a while.'

'Just like womenfolk, Edge,' the boy crowed. 'But you better do what she says.

She's a terror when she's mad. But I guess you know what women are.'

'I guess,' was Edge's dry response.

Her fresh beauty took his breath away. She wore a blue dress under the apron and her hair had been swept up to a golden coil at the crown of her head. For a moment their eyes clashed and colour stormed into her cheeks, but she was soon brusque and businesslike.

'How are you feeling this morning, Mr Tolliver?'

'Pretty fine, I guess, like I told Vern. I'm sorry if I've inconvenienced you, ma'am. But I must have been about all in when you found me.'

'You passed out,' she told him. 'I gave you some brandy and cleaned up the cuts on your face as best I could!'

'I bet I was a pretty sight!'

She asked if he felt like eating some breakfast and Edge assured her he had never been hungrier. He had one qualification to offer, however.

'Can I get up and dress before I eat?'

'Why not take it easy for another hour or so?' she suggested. 'You really did have a bad shaking, whether or not you realize it.'

'I think I do, Miss Wilson... All right, I'll

do as you say. It must be years since I loafed in bed like this. It could get to be a right attractive habit. And please call me Edge, won't you? My full name is Edgeworth.'

'Golly Moses!' the boy marvelled.

'Of course, Edge. My name is Barbara, as you probably know. I've always been known as Barbie.'

'I'm beholden to you, Barbie, and I'm sorry to put you to so much trouble.'

'It's really no trouble at all.'

Her cheeks were becomingly pink as she went out of the room and closed the door behind her. Edge's thoughtful frown deepened when he realized that Vern was still there and that he was chuckling to himself.

'What do you find so ticklish, bub?'

'Heck, I never seen Sis acting up like that before. Why, she was–'

'Saw,' Edge corrected him.

'Oh, sure, I know. Barbie had a swell education, what with all them – those – books and such. She keeps trying to teach me things, reading and writing, and the right way to talk. She wants me to go off to school myself and maybe be a lawyer.'

'I can see a great future for you if you do that,' Edge observed soberly.

'Was it really Caddon's men who gave you

the beating?'

'Who says I got a beating? You've got beating on the brain. I could have fallen off my horse, couldn't I?'

'Call it what you like,' Vern declared with a wisdom that caused Edge to smile in spite of himself. 'But you're not fooling me, Sis neither. She said last night that Caddon must have put some men to trailing you. She said if you'd a grain of sense in your head you'd leave this country and never show your face again.'

'Oh, she did, did she?'

'Sure. But she said you didn't strike her like a man who'd run with his tail tucked between his legs. She said you were the stubborn kind that wouldn't admit you were caught over a barrel.'

'Now you're spinning fairy tales, Vern. Sure there ain't no fairies in the books lying around this house?'

'It's "isn't" and not "ain't",' the boy reminded him with a devil of mischief in his eyes. 'Cross my heart and hope to die, Mr Tolliver. Can I call you Edge? Sis hopes you'll maybe hang around a while and help us run our herd. We've got close on four hundred head of stuff, and it takes a lot of work. Soon as I eat I'll be riding out to look at them. Barbie works as hard as a man. Only I guess you noticed she ain't dressed for riding today. I figure she aims to stay around until you can look after yourself.'

Edge's amused smile faded and he became grave. 'I don't want to put your sister out, Vern. I'll be on my feet in no time at all.'

Breakfast was eggs and crisply fried bacon, with a mound of flapjacks smothered in syrup. Barbie brought it in on a tray and placed it across his knees. She appeared to have shed her earlier diffidence. She looked brisk and in full command of the situation.

'I hope Vern hasn't been filling your head with his nonsense.'

'Vern's grown past the stage of talking nonsense, ma'am. He's next thing to a full-grown man.'

This pleased the youngster who had expected Edge to plead with his sister to take him out of his hair. Vern watched while he ate ravenously, then declared he had better be saddling up. He was excited at the prospect of having Tolliver around the ranch for a while.

'I'll see you when I get back, Edge,' he said. 'You – you'll still be here?'

'You really think I should drift on off this range?'

'I hope you don't. But I wouldn't blame you if you did.'

'I'll think about it,' Edge promised.

Later, the girl brought his clothes in, saying she had cleaned and darned them as best she could. 'You really need a new outfit.'

'I'll get new duds first chance I get. Barbie ... I'm really beholden to you, as you know. But there might be some people dropping by any time to ask if I'm here.'

'Caddon's men.' Her eyes grew stormy. 'It was they who tackled you, wasn't it?'

'Pritch Stevens and a gent called Lem Slater.' He explained about having gone for a swim and of finding the men on the bank when he was about to emerge.

The girl shuddered. 'Lem Slater's no better than a wild animal. He gave Rufe Gates a terrible beating a few weeks back. And I heard he did the same with one of Homer Smith's men.'

The name caused Edge's eyes to narrow. It had been one of Homer Smith's riders who had found his father all those years ago. 'Sounds like a bad egg,' he commented.

'Mark Caddon hired Slater about a year ago,' the girl went on. 'He makes my skin crawl when he comes here sometimes with

Gil–' She broke off while dark colour suffused her cheeks.

Edge's jaw bunched. 'Gil Rimmel?' he prompted. 'You mean that Rimmel calls here sometimes?'

Her head dropped for an instant but then came up. Her eyes sparkled with spirit. She took a long breath, nodded. 'You might wonder why Mark Caddon's men haven't pushed me off Spanish Ridge long ago, why they never interfere with our cattle or bother with Vern...'

'Rimmel is after you?' Edge accused hoarsely. 'But – but do you not object to his–' He realized he was getting into deep water, that this was a subject he should leave strictly alone. On the other hand, he had to find out all he could about the situation. He needed to know exactly what was going on.

Barbie misinterpreted the fire in his eyes. 'It isn't what you think,' she said almost harshly. 'Of course Gil Rimmel rides over here, pesters me into riding with him, to go to the dances in Cedarville with him. But I never go. I would rather make friends with – the devil...'

Her head dropped again and he saw a tear glisten under her eyelid. A wave of relief ran through Edge. He placed the tray on the table at his bedside.

'Why don't you tell him to leave you alone? Why don't you make it plain that you don't want anything to do with him?'

'Oh, you don't understand! If I was downright rude with him he might let the Tumbling C men harass us as they do Rufe Gates and Mr Smith, and the other small ranchers. Maybe the main reason I put up with it is Vern. I've got him to think of, you know. As it is, Vern can come and go as he pleases, and that's the way I want.'

'Of course.' Edge wished he could reach out and touch her arm, her hand, assure her that he would do everything in his power to protect her and her brother from Caddon and his crew. 'But remember,' he felt obliged to add, 'the day will come when Rimmel finds out that his cause is a lost one and that you're just stringing him along. What then?'

'Yes, what then! That's what frightens me. And after watching Gil while he told those lies that could have hanged Rufe Gates, I know that I hate him and everything he stands for. I won't be able to trust myself when he calls here again. I – I might even turn my rifle on him...'

Edge pursed his lips. He rubbed his jaw

and recoiled. He had momentarily forgotten the weals on his face. 'Barbie,' he said slowly, 'do you still need a hired hand? Do you still want me to work for you?'

This seemed to throw her into confusion, and when he demanded to know what was wrong she said unsteadily: 'But, Edge, I've found out that this used to be your home. This ranch was your father's. You could probably claim it even though it was almost a ruin when Dad took it over...'

'Forget it,' he said firmly. 'I don't think I ever wanted to own a ranch anyhow. You might have a stronger legal claim than I have, even if I did want to take it up with the lawyers. Jim Brock was my best friend and anything Jim did is right by me. But I don't see why I can't chip in and help put the old place back on its feet. But I need to be sure you want me around.'

'Of course I do, Mr Tolliver.'

'That's settled then,' he grinned. 'So right now I'm going to get into my boots and do something to earn my keep. If you'll excuse me while I get dressed...'

'But you mightn't be well enough yet,' Barbie objected. 'Shouldn't you wait for another day or so?'

'Horsefeathers, ma'am, if you'll forgive

the expression. I never felt better in my whole life than I do at this minute.'

He took it easy enough in the beginning. He made himself familiar with the lay of the land again. Riding out with Vern stirred a lot of memories. He would have been about Vern's age when he worked with his father. It was true that Barbie Wilson could ride as well as a man, and she certainly had a way with cattle. Edge slept like a log after that first night and was fresh and rearing to go at the crack of dawn. The second and third days were much like the first, and they encountered nothing untoward on all that lush expanse of grass.

On his way home one evening with Vern, the youngster suggested that they make a detour to see how Rufe Gates was making out. Edge thought it a good idea, and they reached the small ranch layout in the soft fragrance of a smoky dusk.

Gates was pleased to meet the man who had saved his life. 'No, I haven't been bothered by Caddon's men again,' he said in answer to Edge's query. He and his wife were beginning to hope that Tumbling C might leave them alone. 'And of course that was a cooked-up deal over the cattle I was supposed to have stolen. I never stole a cow in my life, Tolliver, and that's saying something in cattle country.'

'It certainly is,' Edge agreed.

Gates was able to give them other news. Art Cox had lost something in the region of a hundred head of stock two nights ago. Cox had ridden to Cedarville to complain to Moze Gall, but the sheriff had given him scant satisfaction.

'It's my opinion that Caddon has the law in his hip pocket,' Gates said bitterly. 'With a decent lawman there mightn't be so much rustling.'

Edge took the opportunity to press him further. 'Do you suspect anybody, Rufe?'

'You heard what I said that day at the grain store?' the other countered. 'Well, it still goes. I'm sure that Caddon's own men are the culprits and that Caddon is lining his pockets at the expense of his neighbours.'

Edge told him about the night he had alerted Gard Miller to the raid on his herd. 'It's a pity the cowmen in these parts can't afford to organise a patrol to protect everybody's stock.'

'I'd go along with that any time it's proposed,' Rufe Gates said heartily.

They talked for an hour, and the rancher's

pretty wife insisted on making supper for the visitors. 'I'm glad you're working for Barbie, Mr Tolliver,' she said. 'Barbie can do with all the help she can get.'

Edge suspected that the woman wished to say more. She gave him sidelong looks that made him feel uncomfortable. And then it hit him: Beth Gates wondered if he was aware of the way Gil Rimmel was pestering Barbie. The idea of people thinking that Barbie had any sort of association with Caddon's foreman filled him with wrath. He had an urge to hunt up Rimmel the first chance he got and tell that cold-eyed character what he thought of him. He would also warn him what would happen if he showed his nose at Spanish Ridge again.

At length he and Vern took their leave, saying Barbie would worry if they were too late. Gates shook Edge's hand warmly.

'If ever you think you need me, I'll be ready and waiting,' he promised solemnly. 'You're the kind of man that Mark Caddon and his men can't abide – a fighter. But you'd better remember that they'll go to any lengths to stop you.'

It was something Edge did not have to be told. But he was touched by the man's grit. They left the Gates place and angled over

Spanish Ridge, pushing their horses a little when they came into view of the lighted windows of the ranch buildings.

Barbie was on the porch when they rode into the yard and Edge knew immediately that something was wrong. Closer, the light from the house let him see her pale features more clearly.

'Barbie, what's the matter?'

'Oh, Edge ... Gil Rimmel was here again, not an hour ago. They know that you're here and they warned me to get rid of you at once. Rimmel acted like a mad beast. He said if you're not off the range by morning they'll hound you and kill you. What – what are we going to do?'

TEN

Edge slept badly and greeted a haggard-looking Barbie Wilson at the breakfast table next morning. The girl attempted to appear cheerful in spite of her worry, but her efforts were far from successful. Vern, too, seemed to be slightly depressed. He had little to say while he picked at the food his sister placed in front of him.

Finally, the youngster could stand it no longer and pushed his plate away. He had matured in some strange manner since Edge Tolliver had begun working alongside him. 'Are you going to let that rattler scare you out of the country?' he demanded.

'I've done a lot of thinking about it, Vern,' Edge replied slowly. 'I've tried to figure out what's good for you and Barbie, and what's good for me, and see how both things can be brought together.'

'Sounds like you're trying to join two ropes of different thickness together.'

'Maybe that's just what I'm trying to do. While I'd like to stay on here and work for you and your sister, I don't think it would be wise.'

Vern scowled and glanced at Barbie. 'So they *have* scared you, Edge? They've scared you just the way they scared everybody else. Barbie starts trembling every time she sees Gil Rimmel.'

'That will do, Vern,' the girl chided with reddening cheeks. 'You don't really understand.'

'I understand plenty, Sis,' the boy retorted in disgust. 'But one of these days that Rimmel's going to get a shock when he comes over here.'

'Enough of the war-talk, kid,' Edge admonished roughly. 'That's acting foolish, and you know it is.'

The boy pushed his chair back and swept to his feet. 'All right, Edge. If wanting to stand up and fight is acting foolish, then I don't want to be anything else but a fool. But I figured you were different. I thought you were somebody who'd face Mark Caddon and his men, no matter what they did to you.'

Edge's meagre grin gave his mouth an odd, downward slant. He deliberately avoided Barbie Wilson's penetrating gaze. Whether or not she approved of her brother's behaviour, she was using it to measure the man who had promised to work for her, but who now appeared ready to quit.

'Looks like you might have made a mistake then, kid.'

'Sure looks that way,' Vern rejoined hollowly. He swung and left the room, and Edge filled up his coffee cup, continuing to sip and study the flower pattern on the tablecloth.

He jerked when he heard a horse whistling and then breaking into a gallop. The beast raced away through the front gate. Barbie groaned, dismay adding its stamp to the worry on her features.

'I feared he might do something silly... Edge, where is he off to? He might get hurt...'

'Don't worry. Vern won't do anything but take a hard ride across the country to get his disappointment out of his system. I reckon he's lost his faith in human nature for the time being. I know how he feels.'

'You – you do?'

'Sure.' He began to fashion a cigarette. 'One time I thought my old man was as big as Paul Bunyan, that he could stride over the valleys and mountains like Paul could. The day I learned he was scared of Mark

Caddon was a bad one for me. I guess every kid finds the same old clay feet at some time in his life. He gets over it, though, and later he sees it was a good lesson to learn.'

'Your father was shot. I heard about it. There was a lot of talk, wasn't there, different opinions? It must have been a hard blow.'

'Just about the worst I ever had.'

After breakfast he sat on the porch until he heard hoofbeats approaching from the south. As he expected, it was Vern coming back after kicking his heels in the air. He eyed the youth warily as he brought his pinto horse to a halt. Vern forced himself to look squarely at him.

'I'm sorry, Edge.'

'You don't have to be. The way I see it, you just passed two tests with flying colours. Figure you're ready to do a piece of work?'

The boy's face lit up, then clouded quickly. 'But you said you were leaving...'

Edge tipped his hat up from his forehead. 'I might do that,' he admitted. 'It's about the only sensible thing for me to do. But I can still put in a day's work for your sister. I can come and go, and nobody'll be any the wiser. Nights I can camp over by–' He bit the rest off. It would be better that the boy did not know where he would camp. Then Caddon's men could not pester him to talk.

He wheeled when he realized that Barbie had been listening. 'It really would be the sensible thing for you to do, Edge,' she said gravely. 'You must think of your own safety. You can't afford to give Gil Rimmel the chance to carry out his threat.'

'That's my affair,' he said a trifle curtly. 'Do you want me to work for you? Could you use me around the place?'

'You know perfectly well that I do. But–'

'Forget the rest,' he butted in.

'If you say so. But if you really insist on camping somewhere else at night I'll see that you have enough food to give you breakfast in the mornings.'

'Thank you, ma'am.'

For an instant their eyes clung, and it was Edge who lowered his head first. He left the girl and her brother and headed for the corral to collect his horse. 'I'll be ready when you are, Vern,' he called over his shoulder.

A half-hour after Edge and her brother had ridden off, Barbie was surprised to hear horses thundering in from the north. At first she thought it was Edge and Vern returning for some reason, but when she made out three horsemen approaching steadily an icy hand clutched at her breast and she was obliged to lean against the door-post for support.

The weakness soon passed. She turned into the house, lips compressed determinedly, eyes flashing with intent. She emerged with a rifle that had belonged to her father. The riders were close enough now for her to make out who they were. Gil Rimmel rode slightly in front of the other two, Pritch Stevens and Cash Mayne.

They slowed as they came up to the open gate, and Mayne and Stevens held back while Caddon's foreman pushed on into the yard. Rimmel touched the brim of his hat while his cold eyes swept the ranch environs.

'Good morning, Barbie. Thought I'd pay you another call to see if you delivered my message.'

'I delivered it.'

She noted the way Rimmel jerked on learning that Edge Tolliver had been here. He nodded at the weapon in her hands, smiled crookedly.

'What's the rifle for, Barbie. You afraid of something?'

'Not now,' she replied stiffly, watching the

man's reactions. The cold eyes narrowed while some of the colour receded from his face.

'Are you saying that Edge Tolliver was here?'

'Yes, he was. But he won't be back. It's what you wanted, isn't it?' Her voice hardened and she glanced scornfully at the other two at the fence, slouched over their saddle-horns. 'I can't hire a cowhand because of your tactics, Gil. An honest man is afraid to work for an outfit that could go under the heel of Tumbling C.'

Rimmel clicked his tongue, shook his head in violent rejection of the charge. 'Hard words, Barbie. But I'm sure you don't really mean them.' A slyness crept into his eye, a smugness, as if he had achieved a victory. 'So friend Tolliver decided he'd made a mistake in coming back on to this range?'

'I'm afraid I can't answer that,' the girl replied. 'But he won't be living here, if that's what you mean. He has no wish to bring trouble on my head.'

'Well, isn't that downright gallant of him! Are you trying to tell me that he's still around, that he didn't take my tip?'

'He intends to help me if he can. And why should he leave the Eagle River country when it's really his home? This was his home, you know.'

'Oh, I know well enough.' Rimmel pushed his horse closer to the porch. Barbie fell back a step but raised her rifle.

'Don't come any closer, Gil.'

'Hell's bells, woman! What's come over you? I've always come here as a friend. Why can't we be friends?'

'Aw, cut it out, Gil,' Pritch Stevens broke in. 'The girl can't help it if Tolliver ain't around. Maybe she's just bluffing. Maybe he's halfway out of the territory by now.'

'When I want your opinion, Pritch, I'll ask for it,' was Rimmel's icy response. He eyed the pair with distaste. 'Look, you and Cash ride around for a while and see if you can spot Tolliver. You know what the boss said. If Tolliver doesn't show some horse sense he's finished. All right, get going. I'll follow you shortly.'

Pritch Stevens eyed the foreman for a few seconds, then glanced at the pale-faced girl. He spat deliberately, cuffed his mouth. 'I don't aim to buck you, Gil, but it looks like you're dealing yourself a bad hand. You might be top dog at home, but it don't say you can pester this woman...'

Rimmel spun with a curse, his right hand

150

stabbing for the gun at his hip. He froze when Stevens – having out-drawn him with a lightning-like flick of wrist and fingers – pointed his Colt at the foreman's midriff. A slow, sour grin warped Pritch's cowhand's lips.

'Don't ever try that again, Gil. What in hell do you take me for anyway? Think you can boss me around the way you boss the others?'

'Have sense, damn you,' the foreman blustered. 'That kind of play won't get you anywhere.'

'It'll get *you* dead if you try it again, mister.'

Barbie thought Rimmel would explode with anger, that he would shoot Pritch Stevens in spite of Pritch having the drop on him. The foreman relaxed suddenly, laughed.

'Pritch likes to have his little joke... I'll call past again soon, Barbie, and we'll try to sort things out.'

'You'll be wasting your time,' the girl said steadily. 'If you come pestering me again I'll use this rifle to protect myself.'

'You damn wildcat!' Rimmel erupted in disbelief. 'You're getting pretty sure of yourself, Barbie.'

'Let's get out of here,' Pritch Stevens

snorted. 'Things have come to a bad pass when we have to make war on a woman.'

Rimmel glared at him. He shot a searing look at Barbie, then drew his horse about with a savage sawing of reins and sent it back through the gateway. Stevens and Cash Mayne let him cover a hundred yards or so before going after him.

Barbie watched the three of them until they had gone from sight. The rifle slipped from her hands to the floor of the porch. She gripped the railing until the knuckles of her hands showed white. Finally the strain broke and a tear squeezed itself from the corner of her eye so that the sunlight became a golden blur. Her shoulders began to shake convulsively.

It had gone noon, with a copper orb hanging in the heavens, when the three Tumbling C riders shifted down through a cluster of rocks and saw the two figures in a valley of bluestem below them. Edge Tolliver and Vern Wilson were sharing a meal of beef sandwiches and coffee while their horses grazed nearby on the lush grass. A burst of boyish laughter drifted up to the trio, and Pritch Stevens' jaw hardened. Edge Tolliver was making a joke, entertaining the kid.

Tolliver had been no older than the kid when his old man had gone down beneath one of Pritch's slugs.

John Tolliver had thought he could buck the Tumbling C. Tolliver had been scouting around with his long, suspicious nose turned into the breeze. He had come on a group of Caddon riders with a bunch of Homer Smith's cattle. Tolliver had been making hell-for-leather for Cedarville to tell the sheriff when Pritch had cut him off at Crazy Woman Pass and closed his mouth for ever.

Now his son was poking *his* long nose into Mark Caddon's affairs, and there was only one sure way of stopping him.

'I guessed they'd be around here some-where,' Gil Rimmel mused at Stevens' side. Rimmel had apparently chosen to overlook Pritch's earlier indiscretion, or perhaps he was just biding his time until the moment came to square the deal.

'We've found them right enough,' Cash Mayne nodded, scrubbing his whiskered jaw. He was watching Vern Wilson with a morose glint in his eye. If Pritch Stevens didn't care much for warring with women, he Cash, didn't relish hurting youngsters. 'What do you aim to do now, Gil?' he demanded bluntly.

Rimmel's gaze touched both men, and it was like being touched by twin splinters of ice. 'Only one thing we can do,' he murmured. 'With Tolliver and the boy out of the way the girl will have no option but to clear out.'

'You've changed your mind some, haven't you?' Pritch Stevens nudged. 'All along you've been telling us to leave the Wilsons alone. You said they're just a couple of kids and not worth bothering about. Now you want to kill the boy?'

Rimmel kept his eyes averted. 'It's the best thing to do. We'll fix it so it'll look like Vern and Tolliver had a fight and shot each other.'

'That deal has a sure enough skunk smell, Gil, and you know it,' Stevens countered frostily.

Rimmel locked gazes with the man, and now there was no doubting the hatred swirling in the foreman's cold eyes. 'Since when did you draw the line at shooting somebody, Pritch?' he hissed. 'You got a short memory?'

'Drop it, damn you!'

'No, I won't drop it, mister. Seems you're getting hellish big for your boots. Up to today I've always gotten along pretty well with you, Pritch. Now you've gone high-handed. You figure I need somebody to keep looking over my shoulder and telling me what to do. Well, don't push it too far, my friend. I could have you chased off Tumbling C with your tail down. I could have you fixed up with a rope round your neck the way we fixed Prescott and Langton, and that drifter Morgan we said was rustling when all he was doing was killing a steer for beef...'

'You wouldn't try that, Gil?' Stevens cried hoarsely.

'I damn well might if you don't keep your horns in.'

'We going to fight among ourselves?' Cash Mayne grated. 'Gil, I don't like the way things are going. If we don't get this straightened out I'm going to slope out of here quicker'n hell, no matter about the money we're making from cow-stealing.'

'They're on the move again,' Stevens said sharply, pointing down the valley. 'All right, Gil, what's the jig?'

'The way I said it.'

'Not a chance, mister. And I bet Cash'll back me up. Tolliver's one thing, but killing the kid is something else.'

Rimmel bit his underlip in chagrin. He nodded reluctantly, yielding to the pressure from the other two. 'All right, Pritch, you're still calling the tune. So what about dancing to it?' He gestured towards a rock knob that commanded a good view of the grassland sweeping beneath them, where Edge Tolliver and Vern Wilson were riding along. 'You're the crack rifle shot in the outfit. Go get him.'

'Tolliver?'

'Hell yes. You'll have all the glory to yourself. You'll have wiped the Tolliver clan from the face of the earth.'

Stevens knew that Rimmel expected him to rebel, to argue, and maybe lose his temper. Then the foreman would go back to Mark Caddon and tell him that Pritch had lost his nerve, and it would be a good idea to get rid of him. Sweat shone on the man's brow and he cuffed it away. He stared down the rolling slopes, then took his rifle from its scabbard and climbed the rock ledges until he was on the very nose of the knob. Here, the whole valley swept greenly below him.

Kneeling there with that warm sun on his back, with the brim of his hat tilted to keep any reflection out of his eyes, Pritch Stevens levered a shell into the breech of the Winchester and snugged the stock into his shoulder. A lot of things ran through his mind just then. Once again he saw John Tolliver rock before his bullets, blood streaming down his face. Tolliver dead. He had wondered what it would all mean to the boy. He hated hurting kids just as he hated hurting women. But here was the kid himself, being lined up in his sights. Only he was no longer a kid but a man who could endanger Tumbling C and the rustling forays, and everything else that Mark Caddon's brand symbolised.

A queer mist rose in front of Stevens' eyes. A bead of sweat dribbled down his jaw. The man and the boy down yonder in the bluestem were drawing further away by the minute. He lined Tolliver up in his sights once more, curled his finger around the trigger.

'Hurry it up, Pritch,' Gil Rimmel snarled impatiently. 'You're not getting soft in your old age, I hope?'

Let the bastard ride him, Pritch told himself. Rimmel's days were numbered, if only he knew it. The foreman was bent on destroying him, one way or another. But Gil would not last for much longer, if only he knew it.

Pritch brought the rifle stock into his shoulder where it was as comfortable and as familiar as a well-fitting glove. He took up the pressure once more on Edge Tolliver's bobbing figure.

'Here goes, kid,' he told himself. 'If I don't do this to you now it'll be too late when you find out what happened to your dad.'

Pritch completed the pressure on the trigger. The rifle roared, bucked against his shoulder. At the same time he was thrown forward violently with a searing pain spreading over his back and lancing on through to his stomach.

Down on the rock knob, clawing for purchase with his fingers, striving to drag a breath of air to his lungs, Pritch endeavoured to look over his shoulder to where Rimmel and Cash Mayne waited. Rimmel's smile was the merciless sneer of a vengeful satyr. Smoke still roiled from the six-shooter he had used to shoot him in the back.

ELEVEN

The heavy rifle bullet snapped across Edge's saddle-horn and caused the claybank to jump wildly, and for a split second he was at a loss as to what had taken place. Then the old familiar alarm bells rang as Vern Wilson shouted.

'Watch out, Edge! There's somebody up yonder shooting at us.'

Edge pointed to a hollow. 'Duck in there,' he yelled. 'Fast as you can, kid.'

It seemed incredible that anyone would run the risk of shooting the boy. Edge whirled the claybank to a prancing halt and dragged out his Winchester. He fancied he saw a movement up on the valley rim and sent off two rounds in rapid succession. More gunfire rattled and a rain of slugs slashed the grass around them and peppered the air.

'Look out,' Vern called. 'Get down or they'll kill you.'

It was true, of course. If he remained in the open one of those steel-jackets was bound to find its mark. He was swearing lustily as he pressed his horse towards the hollow where Vern had gone to ground. Here was comparative safety from the would-be killers up in the rocks.

Vern had dismounted and was holding his mount beside a thick clump of brush. He was pale with fright, and beads of sweat stood on his brow. Edge felt sorry for him. Once again he saw a parallel between the youth's existence and his own early life.

'Who do you figure it is?' he asked the youngster.

'Tumbling C, you bet. They sure want to settle your hash, Edge.'

'I reckon,' Edge responded grimly. He cuffed his face, peered up at those rocks flanking the rim of the valley. He should have had more sense than to trust himself below high ground. An army would have spotted the mistake in tactics right away. But how was he to know that Mark Caddon would persist in his merciless hounding?

'If you don't know now you might as well throw in your hand,' he muttered to himself.

'What do you say, Edge?'

'Just talking to myself, I guess.'

The shooting had stopped, and as he searched the rim for sign of movement he thought of Barbie, back there on her own at the ranch-house.

'Do you figure they called at the house again?' Vern queried, as though reading his mind.

'It's just what I'm thinking, kid. They could have stopped off to speak to your sister, find out where I was. Then they must have come looking for me. Well have to get back home *pronto*.'

'I wouldn't worry too much about Sis, Edge,' the boy declared. 'She's got Dad's rifle and she knows how to use it.'

'Wouldn't matter much if that snake Rimmel called again,' Edge gritted. Just thinking about Rimmel filled him with fury.

Vern was studying the rim of the valley where it was flanked by those boulders and rock formations. 'Want to make a run for it?' he queried.

Edge smiled in spite of himself. As far as he could see, there was nothing much up yonder to worry about. The ambushers might have decided to pull out after that initial surprise attack. 'You want to try it? Rats could be waiting for us to show.'

'Let's go.' Vern hauled himself into the saddle. Edge, however, raised a hand for him to wait. He had just seen a horseman moving over one of the long grey ridges that stretched, washboard fashion, to the border of the bluestem.

The rider was intent on taking a northerly direction, away from the valley. He soon went from sight, and no sooner had he vanished than another man on horseback showed. This one rode without much care. Reckless would describe his haste to get away from the rim. He went after the first man and he, too, soon went from sight.

Edge whistled softly, wishing he had a field-glass. 'Doesn't that strike you as almighty queer?'

'You'd nearly think somebody was chasing them,' the boy murmured. 'Wonder what's up.'

'Stay here until I find out.'

Edge left his horse and stepped into the open, rifle at the ready. He stared hard at the rocks that bulked before and above him in the sunlight. It had to be a trick of some kind, of course, and they would nail him as soon as they had lined up clearly in their sights.

Nothing happened. The land was still. Only the distant lowing of cattle came to their ears. Edge turned as Vern hurried out to join him.

'I told you stay where you are. Might be a trick to get both of us where they want us. I figured Caddon and Rimmel would baulk at harming a woman or a youngster, but I've changed my mind about them. They'll kill anybody if it suits their ends.'

Edge brought his horse out of the hollow and mounted. He knew that if he hesitated for a moment longer he would be too frightened to challenge that line of rocks. He reached the shale-littered base without incident and skirted the high end of the valley where he and Vern had halted earlier to eat a meal. He struck a spiralling track that the claybank took in its stride. And when he came out on to a flat bench he halted to cuff sweat from his brow and survey the loftier rims. He was now able to mark the spot where the ambushers had holed up.

He froze suddenly when a trickle of shale poured down almost in front of his nose. The claybank whickered, but he held it on tight rein. Next, it appeared that a miniature avalanche of rock, dust and shale was let loose. He had to draw aside hastily as a particularly large rock missed his head by inches.

He slipped from his saddle and took his horse to the blind side of a large boulder, brought his rifle from the boot and risked a glance down over the valley. He was just able to see Vern Wilson and his horse in the hollow where he had left them. The kid was defying his order and set on coming out of cover.

'Go back!' he yelled. 'Go back...'

He swore, waiting for a burst of gunfire to lift the youngster out of his saddle. Still nothing happened, and this encouraged him to continue his climb to that rock niche where the Caddon ambushers had roosted.

He led the claybank over the last dozen yards, and when he broke over the jagged sandstone lip at last he halted abruptly. A man lay spreadeagled dangerously close to a sheer drop-off. His first thought was that this was an extension of whatever elaborate trick the Tumbling C men were playing. But he soon realized that he might be crediting the Caddon riders with more enterprise than they deserved.

He palmed his Colt and trained it on the figure in the chalky dust. 'All right, mister, you can drop the bluff. If you or any of your pards around here bat an eyelash I'll drill you square.'

No reply. If the man was alive and playing possum he certainly had plenty of nerve.

Vern was climbing quickly, and the cracking of hooves on rock irritated Tolliver. He wanted the silence to continue so that he could concentrate on the immediate scene and try to work things out.

'Did you hear what I said, mister? This is your last chance to save your hide...'

He raised his revolver when the figure moved a little. Then the man groaned. Was he really wounded, and did this indicate that one of his random shots from the hollow had found a mark?

Vern clambered over the rock ledge, and his eyes glittered with excitement when he saw the object of Edge's attention. 'Say, you must have shot one of them...'

Edge had spotted a pool of blood that was fast drying in the sunlight. He pouched his gun and dropped to one knee. The man moved his head so that the side of his face was towards him. The face was lean, terribly drawn, grey in pallor. The eyes reflected his agony. Recognition brought a soft curse to Edge's lips.

'Pritch Stevens! Well, what about this now...'

The eyes tried to bring Edge and the dumb-struck boy into focus. The flat, bloodless lips moved. 'Water...'

Vern hurried to his pinto and secured his canteen. He uncorked it and handed it to Edge. The boy noticed something that Edge had already spotted.

'Looks like he was shot from behind. You couldn't have done it, Edge.'

'Reckon not. Who nailed him then?'

Edge held the neck of the canteen to Stevens' mouth, tipped his head back gently to enable him to swallow. The close-set eyes flickered, flared in recognition.

'Tolliver...'

'It's me, sure enough, Pritch. How come you got yourself into a fix like this? Was it one of that pair we saw hightailing?'

'He – he wanted to shoot the boy.'

Edge's brow wrinkled and he leaned closer to the cowhand. 'You're talking crazy, mister. Whose bullet put you down?'

'Gil... The snake got me from behind. He wanted me to kill you and the boy. But I – I never made war on – kids...'

He went into a spasm of coughing and Edge glanced at Vern. 'Do you figure this the way I see it?'

'Guess so, Edge. It's plain what he's saying. Rimmel told him to shoot me. He wanted both of us out of the way. There's his rifle. He must have fired at you, and then–'

166

'Sure. I get it,' Edge interrupted hoarsely. 'Pritch here slung that first shot at me, and while he was doing it Rimmel plugged him in the back. Well, I never thought Pritch had a white streak.' Another thought struck Edge and he stared at the stricken man. 'Pritch, can you hear me? Listen, I might be able to do something for you if you...'

The colourless lips bent sardonically. 'You can do – something for me, all right, Tolliver. Finish me quick. This pain is – sure – hell.'

'Not that,' Edge objected. 'I really mean I'll do what I can to save you if you answer a couple of questions.' He hurried on while the man was still coherent: 'I'm talking about my father now. John Tolliver. You know who killed him. You know that was no accident. You know–'

Stevens' hard laugh finished up in a spluttering for breath. 'Are you sure you can – take what I'm going – to – tell you?'

'I can take it. Maybe I know who triggered that shot. You, Pritch?'

'I pulled the – trigger right enough. But it was – Mark Caddon who gave the order.'

'Oh, Edge, he killed your dad!'

For a split second Edge was blinded by a wall of poisonous fury. He was rendered

167

incapable of speech. Without really thinking about what he was doing he brought his gun out and eared back the trigger. He pointed the muzzle at a point between Pritch Stevens' eyes. Then the boy had a grip on his arm, was pulling fiercely.

'No, Edge, no!' he panted. 'Don't do it. It'll only make you as bad as him...'

It was incredible that this youngster should have so much wisdom. His grip and his vehement plea had much the same effect as a torrent of cold water. Edge shuddered, shook his head to get rid of the blind, murderous drive that dominated his reason and logic.

'Of course,' he whispered at length, pushing the gun back into its sheath. He regarded Stevens as if he was seeing the man for the first time. If the cowhand feared him, there was no evidence in the bright eyes that glittered on his own.

'Go ahead and finish the job.' His voice was weakening. Blood oozed through his shirt. 'Or haven't you – got the – guts?'

Edge dragged his gaze away. 'Go see if you can find his horse,' he instructed Vern. 'It must be around somewhere.'

Vern went off and Edge squatted beside Stevens to put a cigarette together. Pritch begged for a mouthful of smoke. Edge lighted the cigarette and placed it between the man's lips. The bright eyes mocked him.

'Know your problem, Tolliver?' he whispered. 'You're just too soft.'

'Don't push me, Stevens. I've made up my mind. I'm no mad killer. When Vern gets your horse I'm going to see if I bring you somewhere to get fixed up. Why can't we make a deal?'

'What – sort of deal?'

'Admit that Mark Caddon is behind all this rustling as well as the land-grabbing.'

The other grunted derisively. He began to cough and Edge took the cigarette from him. Vern was gone so long Edge began to fear he was lost, but then he showed, bright-faced, panting with exertion. He had Stevens' grey horse on a rope, and now he fought the fractious beast to trembling standstill.

'What do you aim to do with him, Edge – take him to town?'

'He couldn't make it. No, I think I know where I'll bring him...'

'Jim Brock's place?' the youth hazarded.

'No!' Stevens croaked. 'Not there. Please, Tolliver...'

'You afraid of ghosts, Pritch? You reckon old Jim's shade will be getting restless about now? Maybe he'll start rattling chains when his killer comes back to the scene.'

'Damn you, no!'

It proved tricky getting Pritch aboard his horse. Edge had applied a rough bandage, but it didn't do much to stop the bleeding, and as soon as they had him in the saddle he promptly passed out from weakness.

'He's dead,' Vern pronounced solemnly. But when Edge had a closer look he found that Stevens was still breathing.

Out of the rocks at last, Edge gave the reins of the grey horse to Vern, saying he would ride a little way ahead to scout the country. Edge thought there was a possibility that Rimmel and the other Caddon man were hanging about. Still, if they believed Pritch Stevens was dead they would clear off, hoping to pin the killing on Tolliver. That would strengthen Caddon's case in the eyes of Moze Gall and the other ranchers, and really brand Edge Tolliver as a ruthless gunhand.

Edge hoped that Stevens would stay alive for long enough to admit to murdering John Tolliver and to show everyone that Caddon was running a rustler outfit, had been doing so for years.

He made several halts to check if Stevens

was still alive. Twice Pritch demanded a drink and was supplied with water from Vern's canteen. He was growing steadily weaker, but he still managed to muster a scornful sneer.

'If you think – I'm going to – talk you're crazy. Better – finish me when you – can...'

'Why rob folks of your wit and charm?' was Edge's dry response.

It was afternoon when they came in sight of Eagle Butte. About a half-mile out from the Brock homestead Edge told Verne to haul up and hold Pritch's horse until he got back.

'Want to make sure nobody's holed up there.'

It turned out that the place was deserted, and there was no evidence of anyone having been there since Edge had left. He returned to Vern and they brought Pritch Stevens on up to the front door. Edge carried him inside and laid him on the couch against the wall. Vern brought a basin of water and Edge washed the gunshot wound as best he could, then contrived a bandage. Stevens was conscious during this operation, and while he continued to sneer there was, nevertheless, puzzlement in his eyes.

'I told you you're – wasting your time.'

171

Edge allowed his lips to bend in a thin smile. 'Speaking about time, old son, yours is running out fast. I'm not saying I'll be sorry to see you go, because I won't. The bullet's pretty deep, and I doubt if even the doctor in Cedarville could save you. But you've lived to see the kind of coyote your foreman is. Caddon himself is no better. You think they're going to shed tears over you? Likely Caddon told Rimmel to get rid of you first chance he got.'

'You go – to – hell,' Stevens snarled. He tried to sit up, emitted a moan, and sank back, breathing shallowly. His head sagged and his eyes closed.

'He's done for, Edge.' There was a trace of awe in Vern Wilson's voice.

'Don't figure he is, pard. Pritch is tougher than I thought. He can't last much longer, though. Say, kid, how would you fancy a piece of hard riding in a good cause?'

'You want me to ride to town for the doctor?'

'And Sheriff Gall as well. Feel up to it?'

'Sure thing,' the boy agreed. 'Want me to start right away?'

'That I do, old son. But listen; there might be more Caddon gunhawks hovering around, so watch how you go. When you hit town, tell the doc, then hightail it for Moze Gall and tell him I want him out here real sharp. Tell him Pritch Stevens has admitted to killing my father, and tell him that Gil Rimmel and Pritch must have had a row and Rimmel shot Pritch in the back while he was using me for target practice. Got all that?'

'You bet!'

The youngster hurried outside and swung himself into the saddle of his horse. Another thought had occurred to Edge. He decided on a slight change of tactics.

'Spanish Ridge is on your way. Go there first and get a fresh horse. Tell your sister what happened and tell her not to worry. And, youngster, whatever else you do, mind yourself.'

'Don't worry about me, pard!'

Then he was gone, rounding the corner of the old barn and swinging up a long slope to pick up the Spanish Ridge trail.

When he could no longer see Vern, Edge stripped his claybank and the grey and turned them into the small corral. Then went inside to look at Stevens. Pritch was still alive, but he seemed to be hovering on the brink of the chasm where oblivion waited.

Edge smoked, nervous in spite of trying to tell himself that Barbie's brother would reach Cedarville unscathed. He left the cabin often to patrol as far as the butte, rifle resting in the crook of his arm. He saw the sun slide across the sky and begin its westering course. He kept wondering about Vern. Perhaps he should have left the boy here and gone to town himself. He couldn't get rid of a picture of Gil Rimmel lying up behind a rock somewhere, shooting Vern from his saddle.

Rimmel was a merciless killer who would have to be accounted for soon.

It was close to sundown when Edge heard the drumming of hooves cutting in towards the homestead. He thought he heard Pritch Stevens cackling mockingly as he ducked outside with his rifle.

TWELVE

He recognized Barbie Wilson while she was still some way off. There was no mistaking that trim figure with the hat flying behind her on a chin-strap and her hair billowing in the wind. As soon as Barbie spotted him she called his name, coming on into the front yard at a fast run. She hit the ground while her pony was still on the move. She was dressed in riding skirt, jacket and boots.

'Oh, Edge ... I'm sorry, but I – I just had to come. I've been so worried.'

She came into his arms as if it were the most natural thing to do and he held her close for several moments. She broke away then with a tide of crimson staining her already rosy cheeks.

'Forgive me ... I'm a bit worked up, I guess. After Vern left–'

'So he made it home all right? I sent him on to town. But what happened? Did Caddon's men call again?'

'This morning. Rimmel was furious, Edge. I saw him in his true colours. And if it hadn't been for Pritch Stevens...' A shudder convulsed her. 'I've always detested Stevens, feared him. But if he hadn't taken my part against Gil I don't know what would have happened.'

Edge took her into his arms again. The scent of her wind-blown hair was intoxicating. He never quite knew how he claimed her lips, but he did.

'Oh, Edge...' she murmured with her head buried in his shoulder. 'What is happening to me, to us?'

'Something mighty good, you bet.' He mustered a grin, glanced over the trail to make sure no one had followed her to the homestead.

'Vern told me what happened. You've got Stevens here. Is he – he–'

'Still alive. I reckon Vern told you that Rimmel shot Pritch. Seems there was bad blood brewing between them. Pritch is a queer bird in a way. But, listen, you can't stay here. You must go back home.'

'Please don't force me away,' she pleaded. 'I came because I thought I might be able to help. Shall I see if I can do anything for Stevens?'

'Why not? But I don't reckon you can. Doc might be able to do something. I doubt it, though.'

Pritch was conscious when they entered the house. His eyes widened when he saw who the visitor was. Barbie moved closer to him.

'Is there anything I can do for you, Mr Stevens?' she said gently.

'Miss – Wilson...' the other gulped. 'Well, what about that now?' His voice was little more than a whisper. 'No, I reckon I'm just about – done, ma'am. But you – you watch out for that Gil *hombre*. He's a snake, and he's set on – getting you. And this bird, Tolliver ... He ain't no use neither, girl. Don't trust him.'

Edge grinned tightly and glanced at the girl. She cocked her head to one side, as if considering this.

'Mr Stevens appears to be pretty sensible at the moment, I'd say.'

'Don't you believe it. Pritch just has a way with women. Ain't that so, Pritch?'

'She's too damned good for – any range tramp like you, mister.'

Edge got the lamp going to combat the encroaching shadows. He agreed when Barbie suggested she examine the Caddon man's wound. Edge started to boil water, but the girl demurred.

'Best thing is to let the bleeding stop. We can't do much until the doctor tries to get the bullet out.'

Sweat glistened on Stevens' brow. 'You're wasting your – time,' he objected weakly. His eyes fastened on Edge. 'You're breaking the rules, mister. Are you forgetting I – gunned your – old man?'

Edge's jaw muscles knotted. 'I'm not forgetting anything. You said Caddon told you to do it. That's so, isn't it?'

'Yeah, that's the way – it was.' He was silent for a while, gathering his strength, then he went on: 'Your dad was nosing around, Tolliver. He saw more than he should have seen... He was going to spill the beans to the law.'

Barbie's fingers closed on Edge's arm. 'That's horrible,' she choked.

'Sure, it is,' Edge nodded. 'But I'd rather you heard everything... Pritch, why not come clean about the whole business? You know Caddon's outfit is behind all this beef-lifting. And it's as plain as day that Caddon put Gil up to shooting you after he got you to nail me.'

'You go to hell, mister.'

The talking had tired him and he lay back, his breath hustling noisily. His face was grey, and there was a whiteness about his nose and mouth. Edge sat beside him while Barbie kept going to the door to look out. There was nothing for her to see, but Edge made no comment. She was nervous and restless, and was wondering whether Vern had managed to make it to town.

Edge had already heard the thunder of galloping hooves before she dashed in to tell him that someone was coming. 'Oh, Edge, Vern must have found the doctor and the sheriff...' she burst out.

'I sure hope so.'

A rustle of movement came from the couch and Pritch Stevens raised his head a little. That rebellious glitter was back in his eyes. 'I'm not talking to anybody,' he grated.

While Edge prayed that the newcomers really would be Vern Wilson coming with the doctor and the sheriff, he could not afford to bank on it: it might just as easily be some of Caddon's riders on the prowl. He went outside and closed the door behind him. There was a hint of sage smell in the air. The stars flickered fitfully in the heavens.

The horsemen were angling down from the butte, so it just had to be the Tumbling C men. He swore, shifted on to the corner

179

of the ramshackle barn. He hoped Barbie would have the sense to stay out of sight. He hunkered down, rifle at the steady.

In another few minutes he was able to make out the bobbing figures against the star-flecked sky. There were three in the group, at least, perhaps more. They came to a halt about ten yards out and Edge caught, the low mutter of voices. The leader moved in closer and Edge lined him up in his sights.

'Hold it right there!'

A horse nickered, stamped. Hooves gouged and churned the earth. Then a surprised, gusty curse that told Edge these were Caddon riders.

'That you, Tolliver?'

'It's me, and you're not welcome here.'

'You're taking a lot on yourself, mister. If you've got Pritch in there and he's alive, we want him.'

'So he's no use to you dead, eh? Dead men can't talk, I guess.'

'It was your bullet that brought him down, Tolliver,' another voice rasped. 'Boss says that's enough to keep you in the lock-up for a spell. But we're giving you a chance to save your hide.'

'Now that's downright handsome of you!

What's the deal?'

'Clear out of here now. At once.'

'Well, I can't say I'm ready to do that just yet. Anyhow, Pritch isn't here. What gave you the idea that he was?'

'You're lying in your teeth, Tolliver.'

Edge's eyes narrowed as one of the men broke apart from the other two. As far as he could make out, there was just the three of them. The man began to sidle his horse to the rear of the main building.

'I told you to stay where you are,' Edge rapped. 'All of you.'

'Get him, boys!'

Three revolvers boomed from three different angles. They had separated quickly, but all their bullets converged in the general direction where Edge crouched, whining away into the night, slapping into the walls of the house itself. Edge drew aim on a shifting form and fired. He saw his target leap up in his saddle, back arched. A spine-chilling yell added to the general din. The man fell across his mount's neck and the beast bounded away, trumpeting furiously.

The remaining pair broke back a little, emptying their short-guns, and then resorting to their rifles. Edge splashed a hail of .30-30 stuff around them. He heard someone call from the front of the house – Barbie. He shouted at her to keep out of sight. The rifles of the intruders bellowed again and again. The night was pocketed with crimson. Cordite filled Edge's nostrils.

He was setting himself to shift on over to the front porch when another sound lifted above the racket of prancing hooves and gunfire and defiant shouting. More horses were pounding in towards the homestead, these angling from the direction of Spanish Ridge. Iron-shod wheels struck an incongruous note, bouncing and lurching as they shortened the distance. A high-pitched hail reached his ears.

'Edge, are you there?'

Edge held his breath, jacking another shell into the breech of the rifle. How many rounds had he left – one, two? He resisted the temptation to glance at the new arrivals; instead, he watched where the two Caddon raiders were tearing back into the night shadows.

'Edge, is that you?' Vern Wilson called.

'It's me.' He felt like laughing hysterically.

Barbie emerged from the house again as Doc Benfleet's buggy rolled up to the front of the building, the two team horses snorting and blowing. Moze Gall was here as well, on a wild-looking plug. Another rider materialised, and this one Edge recognized as Gall's deputy, Bob Lacey.

'What was all that shooting about?' Gall wanted to know. 'Tolliver, in all my damn life I never met a man like you. Were you born in the middle of a hurricane?'

'Coyotes sneaking around, Sheriff. I think I hit one of them.'

'Well, Edge, you can see I made it after all,' Vern Wilson exulted. 'Is he still alive?'

'Just about,' his sister told him.

Edge took the medico's bag and helped him to the ground. Benfleet was grouchy at the best of times, and it was evident that the journey from town had made him testier than usual. He grunted something and grabbed his bag.

'Where's the patient?'

'Inside, Doc. He's all yours.'

Moze Gall clutched Edge's arm as he was about to follow the medico into the house. There was the faintest reek of whisky from the sheriff.

'What was all that shooting about? I want the truth.'

'Caddon's boys. I'm sure it was. I think one of them was Pinto Gahan. I recognized Rimmel's voice. It was Gil who drilled Pritch in

183

the back.'

The lawman stared at him. 'I wish I knew where this is going to finish, mister.'

Edge had just about reached the end of his tether. 'I'll tell you,' he said flatly. 'It'll finish when Caddon and his toughs are put where they belong – in jail or under the ground. And here's something else for you to chew on, Sheriff: Pritch admitted to killing my father.'

'The hell you say! But – but–'

'Barbie Wilson was a witness. I asked Vern to bring you here so you might get the chance to hear the whole story. But Pritch only talks when he's got a mind to.'

'So what do you hope to gain?' Gall's tone was tinged with irony. His deputy stood back in the shadows, watching and listening. 'It'll take more than a confession from Stevens to bring Mark Caddon to his knees. A lot of others have tried it.'

'You bet they have! Including my father. He was trying to get to town to see you the day he was murdered. He'd overheard something about a rustling deal.'

'That's just as maybe,' Gall grunted. He wanted to get inside the house. 'You don't know that. Nobody knows.'

Something snapped in Edge and he

grabbed the lawman by the front of his shirt. A hard heave sent Gall slamming against the doorjamb. Edge might have hit him had Deputy Lacey not jammed his gun against his ribs.

'Ease up, buster, or I'll plug a hole in you.'

Edge paid no heed. 'Sheriff, there's one thing I've got to know: are you drawing pay from Caddon?'

'You're loco–'

'Are you, damn it?'

'What gave you such a notion? Take your hands off me. I'll throw you into jail so fast you won't know which day it is.'

'I'll put it this way,' Edge pursued relentlessly, 'will you go after Caddon if you're certain he's a thief and a killer, or a man who hired others to do his killing?'

'Hell yes!' Gall exploded. 'It's my job. But you're away off the mark, Tolliver. You've got this bee in your hat about Mark Caddon ... look, I came out here to see Stevens. Is he here or isn't he?'

They moved on in to where Doc Benfleet was closing his bag with almost savage deliberateness. A line of sweat glistened on the bridge of his boney nose. His necktie was awry.

'Would you like a cup of coffee, Doctor?'

Barbie was asking him in a strained manner.

'No, thank you, Miss Wilson. Perhaps I can be permitted the observation that I'm surprised to find a girl like you mixed up in a mess like this.'

Edge gaped from Barbie to the medico. He felt a sudden constriction in his chest. 'You mean he's dead, Doc?'

'That about sums it up,' the medico agreed drily. He adjusted his hat and glanced at Moze Gall. 'Pritch Stevens talked to Miss Wilson, Sheriff,' he announced. 'She can tell you what he said. This really is an affair for the law.'

'What's that supposed to mean?' Gall demanded while his eyes snapped nervously.

'Barbie, what did he say to you?' Edge queried. 'Did he say anything about…'

The girl nodded. There was pain in her eyes, shock. But then a glimmer of gladness, and something like triumph, showed.

'What did he say?' Moze Gall asked. He gestured to his deputy to stand by the door and stay on the alert.

'He told us – the doctor and me, that is – that Mark Caddon has been a cow-thief for most of his life, that he built up his ranch to what it is by stealing stock, by altering brands, and selling to markets where no

186

questions were asked. He also said that Caddon has planned a raid on Art Cox's herd...'

'When is this supposed to take place?' Gall said raggedly.

'Tomorrow night.' Barbie's eyes found Edge's, clung. She could see a long shudder run through the tall man. His mouth trembled in a smile.

'Well, I guess it was worthwhile trying to save Pritch after all,' he said. 'But it must have been your influence that did the trick, Barbie.'

Moze Gall looked stricken. He had gone very pale and he looked around the room with a sort of desperation in his eyes. Edge wondered if he was going to show a yellow streak at the last minute.

Gall was appealing to Doc Benfleet who had managed to load a pipe with tobacco and get it going. 'I don't want to rope you into anything, Doc. But I've got to know if what the girl says is true. You heard it?'

'Every word,' Benfleet droned. He added disapprovingly: 'I'm not in the law business at all, Moze, but I've always had doubts about Mark Caddon. What other society and what law office would countenance a man being hanged without a proper trial and a just verdict?'

Gall turned away from him, muttering something that sounded like an excuse. The medico was not finished with him.

'Far be it from me to tell you your job, Moze, but if I was wearing your badge right now I'm afraid there would be only one course of action open to me...'

'I know how to do my job, damn it.'

'Dare say you do.'

The sheriff went over to consider the dead Stevens for a minute, then he fixed Edge Tolliver with a hard stare.

'Looks like you're getting what you want at last, mister.'

'All I want is fair play, Sheriff. Not only for me but for all the honest ranchers in the territory.'

'Amen to that!' Doc Benfleet intoned. He moved towards the door and Deputy Lacey stepped aside. 'What about it, Moze? I'm sure there are plenty of people back in town who would be only too willing to help if you're thinking in terms of a posse.'

'I'll wait until morning to see Caddon,' Gall almost snapped at him. 'Soon as it's daylight I'll head for the ranch.'

'You'd better do more than just see him, Sheriff,' Edge said bitingly. 'If you don't do your duty now you'll stand to lose that piece of tin on your shirt.'

They all thought Moze Gall would strike Tolliver for that. He did take a quick pace towards him, but was halted by the look in the younger man's eye.

'I don't mean to ride you, Sheriff. Just make sure you do what you're supposed to do. Me, I'm right behind you all the way. But, tell me something,' Edge went on curiously, 'did you never suspect that Caddon was bringing you into his spider's web for his own ends?'

Gall's lips framed a hot retort, but he swallowed thickly instead, lowered his gaze. He had the grace to look guilty and embarrassed.

'No,' he sighed at length. 'I never did. I just thought he was a stickler for law and order. I know the lynchings were all wrong, but lynching has proved the best way to make law-breakers think twice. Maybe I should have bucked him earlier. But I always saw him as a help to my cause rather than a hindrance.'

Doc Benfleet released a cloud of smoke at the ceiling, placed a hand on Moze Gall's shoulder. He signalled for the deputy to open the door for him.

'I'll see you to your rig, Doc.'

'Thanks, Bob.'

The two men went outside and Moze Gall was left with Edge, Barbie, her brother and the dead man. A little bitter smile hovered around the lawman's lips.

'I guess I'd better get back. What do you aim to do with the body?'

'It'll be in the barn when his pards want to collect it. And, Sheriff, if you need any help...'

Moze Gall pushed his way outside without answering. One thought was uppermost in his mind just then – settling the score with the man who, all these years, had taken him for a gutless fool.

THIRTEEN

Dawn found Moze Gall out and about in Cedarville, restless, peevish, challenging man or beast to dare look him squarely in his bloodshot eyes. He hadn't slept much and his head buzzed. A younger man might not have been fooled so easily by Mark Caddon, that thieving, murdering son of a bitch who had kept him under the thumb of intimidation for so long, laughing up his sleeve at him, sneering at him behind his back. It was a wonder Caddon hadn't thrown him a bone now and again so that he might impress on him that he really belonged in the dirt.

If Caddon had been rustling and manipulating people for his own advantage for years – ever since Edge Tolliver was a kid – then he had been a blind, pliable tool in the hands of a master schemer.

Deputy Bob Lacey was brewing coffee on the stove in back when Gall returned to his office. He drank a mug of the hot, black stuff, and felt a little better afterwards. Lacey hunted up the broom and turned towards the empty three-cell block. He pretended not to notice that the sheriff looked as if had spent the night in the company of ghosts.

'What you aiming to do, Moze?' the lean, middle-aged man ventured as he gave the broom a couple of tentative passes around the scarred desk that was littered with papers browned with the heat and the daylight. 'You really planning on going out there?'

Gall was pouring a second mug of coffee. He sat down and pulled a drawer open, raked out a box of .45s, glanced over at the wall rack where half a dozen Winchester rifles were chained into their slots.

'Sure, I'm going, Bob. No other option. I've never thought much about my standing in this burg until recently. I've let things drift, I guess. Maybe turned blind eyes now and again. But this bird Tolliver has made me take a new look at things. So has that Wilson girl and the doc. Benfleet can chew up a lot of words when he gets going, can't he?'

Lacey was more interested in what might ensue when Moze had ridden into the front yard at Tumbling C.

'What do you plan to do when you get there, Moze?'

'Well, now, let me see...' The sheriff's

laugh held a trace of irony. 'Guess I'll feel obliged to tell Mr Caddon what I think of him. Then I'll ask him to ride into town with me.'

'Reckon he'll come? What if he thumbs his nose at you? Can you see him surrendering to the law, facing rustling charges, murder charges?'

'He'll come,' was the stony response. 'Caddon has led me around by the nose for quite a spell, Bob. Now it's my turn.'

'Will you mention the raid on Cox's herd tonight that Pritch is supposed to have talked about?'

'I'll keep that up my sleeve. If I get Caddon to town there shouldn't be any raid at Cox's.'

The deputy decided the cell block would do without cleaning for another day. He put the broom away and pulled his hat on, turned to the door. 'I'll get the horses ready.'

'Just mine, Bob,' Gall told him. 'Yeah, I mean it. I'm going alone. You hold down the office until I get back. If I'm not home by dark get a couple of fellas and come after me. *Sabe?*'

'But you can't go out there on your own,' Lacey objected. 'Tackling that outfit single-handed would be a crazy move. If Rimmel really killed Stevens – and it appears that he did – he'll kill again if Caddon tells him. Look at the hardcases that bird hires – Pinto Gahan, Mayne, that Lem Slater...'

'Go get my nag, Bob. I want to hit the trail before Tolliver takes it into his head to make a one-man stand against Tumbling C. He would, too, the darned fire-eater!'

When his deputy had left the livery the sheriff checked his revolver and carefully replaced the shells he had wiped. The box of .45 stuff would go into a saddlebag. Next, he brought a rifle from the rack and examined the mechanism. All this took him back to a long-ago day when he had made another lone trip like the one in the offing. A roughneck had slit a man's throat and lit out for the border. That trail had taken him clear to El Paso, where he ran the killer to earth and planted three bullets in him while he was trying to drag his gun out.

They were good days too, Moze Gall reflected. He had stood man-high, and was tough, aggressive and a totally independent enforcement officer. In those days he would never have countenanced a public hanging without a proper trial, such as Caddon had gotten away with.

What had come over him he wondered?

How had he let himself slide into this comfortable but potentially dangerous rut?

He stirred when he heard Bob Lacey pulling his horse to a standstill outside. He joined Lacey and pushed his rifle into the scabbard before mounting up. Once again the deputy offered to go along with him or to round up a posse of reliable townsmen.

'No, Bob. I reckon this is the best way.'

'Good luck, Moze.'

Then he was riding down the dusty street that was in the process of coming to life. News of Pritch Stevens' death had reached town via the doctor, and this had provided the spark that set other rumours alight. It was argued that Mark Caddon's outfit had been mixed up in shady deals. Rustling and murder were mentioned in the same breath.

Moze Gall travelled due north through the morning sunshine. He reflected that it had been quite a while since he had gone riding like this on his own. He had missed out on a lot, he supposed, and but for the worry on his mind and the weight of authority he carried on his shoulders, he would have gained a certain enjoyment from the chirping and fluting of birds in the trees and thickets that he passed. The grass was green and long, the sage almost purple where it swept off in the distance. The wild flowers appeared to smile and perform a graceful dance in the breeze for him.

When he reached a spot where he knew he was, roughly, on a parallel with Spanish Ridge and that beyond there he might find Edge Tolliver camping at Jim Brock's place, he felt a little yearning for companionship. Even Tolliver had his good points, and in a way he couldn't help admiring him. And wasn't Edge Tolliver the sort of man he would like to have at his side in a fight? Wasn't Tolliver the kind of man he had once been himself?

He tried brushing these thoughts aside, labelling them as signs of weakness. If the person who professed to symbolise and support the rule of law could not stand on his own legs and perform his own chores, then it was time he was tossing his tin badge into a drawer.

He was on Tumbling C grass, with cattle scattered in their hundreds on every side, when he glimpsed a horseman coming over a distant ridge. He dragged his mount to a halt, certain that the rider had spotted him and would come this way. He saw the man draw something from a saddle-pouch and hold it to his face, a spy-glass. After a long, steady regard, the horseman swung around and vanished behind the ridge.

The sheriff dragged his hat off and ran his elbow around the sweatband. His lips peeled away from his teeth in a grimace of annoyance. The sun was gathering strength, and Moze studied the lay of the land, wondering if it was conceivable that he might be in danger out here. The notion angered him, and he pushed his horse into a run, eager now to reach Caddon's ranch and get this errand over with. For the first time he questioned the wisdom of leaving Bob Lacey behind in town.

It was nearing noon when he topped a rise and saw the long sprawl of the Tumbling C buildings outlined against the sky. He had gone another quarter-mile when two riders angled away from the ranch, then switched course so that they would cut him off.

An odd chill settled along the sheriff's spine when he picked out the figure of Gil Rimmel. The foreman's companion was Cash Mayne. Rimmel greeted him with gruff cheerfulness.

'Morning, Mr Sheriff! You must have left town pretty early.'

'Early enough.' Gall didn't like his manner or his tone. It was as if Rimmel was secretly laughing at him. What did these men really think of the law as represented by fat, whiskered Moze Gall? Not a whole damn lot, he was certain.

'Where you heading for, Sheriff?' Mayne wanted to know. Mayne reminded Gall of a snake on the look-out for a rabbit.

'To see your boss. Is Mark at home?'

'Reckon so, Sheriff,' Rimmel said with that sly emphasis on the "Sheriff" tag. 'Must be something pressing on your mind?'

Moze Gall refused to favour him with an answer. He didn't like the foreman's tight smile. It was as good as saying: '*Well, here we've got you on home territory, buster. What use do you think that tin star is out here?*'

Gall pushed his horse on towards the ranch buildings and, as he half expected they might, Rimmel and Mayne fell in on either side of him. They rode into the big front yard like that. The whole place had an air of industry: horses stamping somewhere, a man shouting, two others arguing over something or other – both out of sight. The smithy's hammer was clanging away in the forge.

Moze dismounted and worked his legs to get some of the stiffness and cramp out of them. He let the fingers of his right hand fall to the butt of his gun in an instinctive motion he was not even aware of. In a way it was like the old times before he grew fat and let himself slow down, before, too, he had allowed himself to slip into the cocoon that was the town of Cedarville with the merchants' ingratiating nods and smiles, and the indifference of the cowhands who drifted in from the various outfits. He had become almost like an ornament in that town, something folks knew was always there … like a familiar picture hanging on the wall, or an old whiskered hound dog that had no sense of smell in its snout any more.

'Reckon you can find your way on in?' Rimmel said with a little dip of his hawk's head and that cold smile playing at his lips.

'You go tell Mark to come out here, Gil.'

'Say, this sounds hellish ominous, Moze!'

The sheriff felt his teeth coming together. He remembered when he would have wiped the yard with Rimmel for that sort of remark.

As it turned out, there was no need for the foreman to summon Mark Caddon. The rancher appeared on the porch as if he had been hanging back in the corridor, watching and waiting. Moze Gall noticed that Caddon evinced no surprise at his arrival. He recalled the watcher with the telescope.

'Howdy, Moze,' Caddon greeted with a

short laugh. 'Don't stand there with your mouth open like a fish. Come in, come in, old friend!'

Damn him, the sheriff thought. The only friend he'll ever find will be on the other side of hell's hinges. He shook his head, deciding this might be the last chance he would have to prove something to himself.

'This isn't what you'd brand a social call, Mark,' he said in a measured tone. 'In fact, you could say that my business is pretty serious.'

'Well, I'd already assumed that much!' Caddon's eyes twinkled with gentle mockery. 'But why stand out in the heat? Has that Tolliver tramp been cutting up again?'

'It's to do with Tolliver right enough. You too, I guess. And Gil there as well...'

'Then you'd better spit it out, old-timer.'

'Reckon I'd better.' Gall cleared his throat, let his eyes settle defiantly on the still-mounted Gil Rimmel and Cash Mayne before switching back to Caddon. 'Mark, I must ask you and Gil to accompany me back to Cedarville.'

'What! Moze, you sure the sun hasn't got to your head?'

'Sun's got nothing to do with it,' the sheriff said doggedly. Strangely, all his earlier apprehension seemed to have evaporated like mist under heat. He saw this as nothing more or less than a job to be got over and done with as soon as possible. 'You see, Mark, I've come out here to arrest you and Rimmel.'

'He's gone crazy,' Gil Rimmel breathed. He had paled, and now he came out of his saddle. Cash Mayne followed suit.

'Crazy or drunk,' Mark Caddon thundered. The swift, unthinking anger he was capable of took over. 'Moze, I'm not particularly fond of that kind of joking...'

'It's no joke, Mark. Maybe I've let you run away with the idea that I'm some kind of soft mark that can be walked over at will, or bought for a few drinks. Maybe, too, I've been inclined to fool myself that you and your outfit couldn't possibly be involved in anything underhand–'

'But we're not, curse it!'

'I'm afraid I think otherwise,' Gall said steadily. 'Anyhow, that's all over and done with. I happen to know you're a rustler. I guess you've been stealing other people's cows from the very start. I know that Rimmel here killed Pritch Stevens–'

'Tolliver shot Stevens,' Rimmel grated. 'Cash can bear me out.'

'Cash needn't bother. You see, Pritch lived long enough to talk plenty. He spilled the beans about this outfit. He said that Mark–'

And that was as far as he got before Rimmel's nerve broke and he went for his gun. But it was a move that Moze Gall was ready for and had been waiting for. His own revolver leaped to his fingers, cocking the hammer in a single, smooth action.

'Try it and you're dead,' he told Rimmel quietly.

The foreman withdrew his hand as if the handle of his Colt was red-hot. He gulped, glancing at the half-bent figure of his boss on the porch. Mark Caddon favoured him with a scornful glare.

'You'll regret this, Moze,' Caddon hissed at the sheriff. 'You've come out here with the wildest story I ever heard.'

'You'll get your chance to deny it, Mark. Not at Needham's grain store, I might tell you,' Gall added thinly. 'From now on everything's going to be done legal and proper in this neck of the woods. Proper hearing, proper procedure. Jury, if one's needed.'

'Why, you fat toad! I'll see you in Hades for this.'

'Don't brag too loud, Mark.' Gall raised his gun a little. 'Are you coming with me?'

Caddon started a furious protest, but then he breathed hard down his nostrils. His head rolled and he dipped his chin a couple of times. 'Very well, Moze,' he said constrainedly. 'If you're really set on going through with this farce I'll humour you. But I'll do it in my own way, and you can like it or lump it. I've nothing to fear from you or anybody else on this range. You head back to town and I'll follow presently. Give me a couple of hours.'

The sheriff thought this over for a moment. Even though he had come out here determined to return with Caddon and Rimmel, he had gained a victory of sorts. He would give Caddon a day, and if he failed to keep his word he would return to the ranch with a properly sworn-in posse.

'What have you got to lose, Sheriff?' Cash Mayne prodded. 'If the boss doesn't show up you'll know where he's at.'

'What do you say, Gil?' Gall directed at the grim-faced Rimmel. 'You'll ride in of your own free will with Mark? And remember, you'll get every chance to state your case.'

Rimmel threw a sidelong glance at Mark Caddon and Caddon's nod of agreement was barely perceptible.

203

'I've got nothing to lose,' the foreman grunted. 'It's our word against the range tramp's. That's what it boils down to.'

'Then you'll come to my office?' Gall prodded.

'I said I would, damn it! Want me to sign something in my own blood?'

Moze Gall's whiskered cheeks coloured, but he decided not to let them ruffle them. 'I hope to see you before sundown,' he said, lowering the hammer of his gun and restoring the weapon to its pouch. 'If you haven't turned up by morning I'll come out after you.'

'With a posse?' Mark Caddon jibed.

'Any steps I take will be legal and proper,' Gall rejoined curtly.

He swung himself back into his saddle and turned his horse across the yard. He was aware of an unusual silence about the ranch layout just then. A stableman over yonder by the corner of the barn stood glowering at him. An elderly lame cowhand who filled in as wrangler when the occasion demanded had stationed himself at the edge of the patio where bees buzzed among the flowers and where a cunningly constructed fountain sprayed water unfailingly, whatever the weather.

Going through the gateway, Moze Gall wished he could rid himself of the chill that had settled on his backbone. Although it was overpoweringly warm by then, the lawman felt cold all over.

Mark Caddon spoke after him.

'Why not get something before you ride back, Moze? You sure look like you could do with a couple of drinks.'

Another goad with a sharp spur! Gall half-turned and lifted his left hand. 'No, thanks, Mark. I'm in a hurry.'

'Bet he is!' he heard Cash Mayne crow sneeringly. 'Damned old windbag must have got nerve from some place.'

'Out of a bottle, most likely,' Gil Rimmel observed in a voice raised to carry.

A long shudder ran through the lawman, and he knew that by putting his back to them he was taking one of the biggest risks of his life. But he must not weaken at this juncture, must not let them push him into doing anything that could be construed as weak or foolish.

Clear of the Tumbling C headquarters, he raked his mount's flanks with unaccustomed roughness. He had made up his mind to veer towards Eagle Butte and tell Edge Tolliver what he had done. If Tolliver wasn't at Jim Brock's homestead he would almost certainly find him at the Wilson place on Spanish Ridge. Having taken an uncompromising stance against Caddon, he wished to keep a tight rein on Tolliver for the time being. The last thing he wanted right now was for Tolliver to spread his war talk among the other ranchers. The law officer in Cedarville would have its hands full during the next day or so without Edge Tolliver complicating things.

The miles passed under the plodding hooves of his horse. The brittle sunlight beat down on his shoulders, brought salt sweat to his forehead and cheeks, to the corners of his mouth. The cold had long since melted out of his bones, and he was feeling more like his old self. In fact, he was feeling better now than he had felt in a very long time.

'Maybe the old dog hasn't forgotten how to howl after all,' he mused indulgently.

He passed out of the strong rays of the sun into the dark shadows flung by the rims of a small, narrow-walled canyon. And that was when a rifle cracked and the world seemed to splinter into a million shards of blinding light.

FOURTEEN

Edge Tolliver arrived in Cedarville to learn from Deputy Bob Lacey that he had missed Moze Gall by a mere half-hour. The sheriff had insisted on making the trip to Tumbling C alone. The news surprised Edge. He was even more surprised when Lacey told him that Gall intended bringing in Mark Caddon and his foreman Rimmel, to stand trial for rustling and murder.

Edge studied the deputy for a moment, wondering if the sheriff had not bluffed him and everyone else by pretending to go after Mark Caddon while, in reality, he was making tracks out of the country before things got too hot for him.

Bob Lacey appeared to read his mind. 'You don't reckon Moze might have the nerve to do that, Mr Tolliver, eh?'

'What's *your* opinion, Deputy?' Edge countered. 'You know him longer than I do. But I recall when he used to tag along at Mark Caddon's tail. I used to think Caddon had him tucked away in his bill-fold.'

'Then you thought wrong.' Lacey had a harried look about him. He kept going to the office window and peering along the road when he heard a horse or wagon going past. 'Moze'll bring them in all right. He's cottoned to the fact that the Tumbling C boss has been using him all these years. When he found that out he went madder than blazes.'

Edge grew sombre. He turned to the doorway. 'If he felt like that he should have asked for help. Don't you know what they're liable to do to him out there? That pack of coyotes will kill anybody who tries to brace them.'

'Well, maybe I should have followed him. But he said–'

'You sure as hell should have followed him, Deputy.'

Edge was mounted and pulling his clay-bank around in the road when Lacey came out behind him. He looked frustrated, annoyed over what Edge had said.

'Sheriff doesn't want any interference, friend. And he's not going to tell Caddon about the raid on Cox's place that Pritch Stevens spoke of.'

'Makes no difference,' Edge grunted. 'But don't worry about me spoiling the sheriff's style. It's the last thing on my mind.'

Riding down the street, Edge kept a sharp look-out for evidence of Tumbling C men in town. He had ridden into Cedarville to ask Gall if he intended doing anything about Mark Caddon. And if the sheriff had intended bearding the cowman in his den, he expected him to have a posse along to back him up.

He pushed his claybank hard in what he knew would be a vain effort to overtake the sheriff. Moze would have had too great a start on him. He saw ample sign of the lawman's passing, but reached the boundary of Caddon's grazing land without spotting him. Edge reined in at this point, knowing that to press any further would be to invite disaster. After all, if Gall wanted to play the game his way he had every right to do so. And Moze was old enough and experienced enough to take care of himself. If, for any reason, the sheriff's real intention was to warn Caddon or throw in with him, then he, too, would be caught up in the tide of retribution that must swamp Tumbling C eventually.

The flat crack of a rifle being discharged caused Edge to stand up in his stirrups and search the distance on all sides. The shot had come from far to the south and west – the direction of Eagle Butte! Edge swung out for Jim Brock's place, wondering what was going on. The sun's rays increased in intensity as he galloped over hill and hollow. Then the seemingly endless sweep of grass and sage was in front of him. His narrowed eyes picked up a running horse with a man hanging slackly in the saddle.

The drumming of the claybank's hooves appeared to frighten the other horse and it disappeared into a long dip that ran off to the North Fork of the Eagle. Edge had to squeeze every ounce of speed and stamina out of his mount in order to head off the runaway.

He cornered it in a boulder-strewn pocket as its rider tilted sideways and dropped to the earth in a loose heap. Edge was suspicious at first, but he soon realized that the man was genuinely hurt. Likely he had been that rifleman's target. He moved in closer and came out of leather, and suddenly his heart gave a sickening lurch. The wounded man was none other than Sheriff Moze Gall. The heavy bullet had smashed into his right shoulder and his face was drawn with shock and pain. He tried to get his gun out when Edge bent over him, but then he recognized the tall man. He sighed heavily.

'Thank heaven it's you,' he panted. 'What are you doing out here?'

'Hoped to overtake you. Your deputy told me where you were going. Did you visit at Tumbling C?'

Gall's lips twisted in a little bitter smile. 'Yeah ... I called on Caddon. I didn't mince words with him. Say ... take my scarf and make a pad for the bleeding.'

Edge did the best he could for him. He wiped the lawman's streaming brow and whiskered cheeks.

'What did you say to him?' he queried.

'Told him the game was up. Told him he was a rustler and a killer, and he'd better come back to town with me.'

'You're one hell of a star-packer, Sheriff. But they drilled you instead?'

'No ... Mark agreed to ride into town later with Rimmel. He claimed they had nothing to fear or be ashamed of. I took him at his word and rode away. Somebody must have followed me...'

'Bet your life they did! They never intended you to get back to town alive, Sheriff.'

Edge caught the lawman's horse and managed to get him back into the saddle. 'Hold on as best you can. But you can't make it to town in that shape.'

'Where else can I go, damn it,' the other grumbled.

'Spanish Ridge.' Edge's tone invited no argument. 'Barbie can look after you while Vern heads to town again for the doc. Vern can tell your deputy what happened.'

Moze Gall was in no shape to protest, even had he wished to. They moved off, bearing towards Spanish Ridge.

Barbie and her brother spotted them as they wound in through the yard gate. Edge lost no time in explaining what had happened. Moze Gall was helped into the house and made comfortable. Edge took the goggle-eyed Vern by the sleeve.

'Head for Cedarville, pard. Bring the doctor and Deputy Lacey. And watch how you go.'

'Sure thing, Edge. But you ain't thinking of tackling the Tumbling C crowd on your own?'

'Not on my own.' He headed outside again, and Barbie hurried after him. He had never seen anyone look so concerned.

'Edge, I'm scared. Where – where are you going? What are you trying to do?'

'Don't worry, honey. I'll be fine.' He kissed

her quickly on the cheek and took his clay-bank on round to the corral. He switched his saddle and gear to a roan, and was soon cutting back towards the north.

He rode more warily now, thinking of Moze Gall being bushwhacked. This was evidence enough that Mark Caddon was prepared to stop at nothing in his bid to hold on. Caddon's whole future – his very life – hung in the balance now, and he would fight with the savagery of a wolf to retain what he had. There was another thing to consider: if the bushwhacker had any doubt about his bullet killing the sheriff, he could very well be skulking around Eagle Butte.

Edge rode steadily for a while and then entered a canyon that would give him quicker access to the higher range. He was almost through the sprawl of cliffs and boulders when he saw movement on a rock bench on his left. Sunlight glinted on metal, and even as the significance registered a rifle opened up and a bullet whistled over the roan's head. Edge glimpsed a man on horseback and palmed his revolver. He triggered two shots, realizing that he had caught the ambusher in the act of crossing the canyon, probably to travel on down to Eagle Butte.

The horse up yonder appeared to stumble.

213

Its rider whipped his rifle around, not taking time to aim. The weapon thundered and the heavy steel-jackets thrummed harmlessly into the ground. Edge held his Colt across the crook of his left arm and fired, once, twice, three times. He was rewarded with a gurgling cry. A torrent of shale preceded the man's overbalancing in his saddle and pitching down among the rocks.

Edge left the roan to clamber through the boulders. He reached the cleft where the bushwhacker lay in a broken heap, eyes staring glassily at the heavens. Gil Rimmel.

Edge returned to the roan and levered himself into leather. He raked the beast's flanks until they were out in the open once more, and now he set his sights on Gard Miller's Triangle M. This was his goal before making his next decisive move – a visit to Mark Caddon's Tumbling C. It was time to enlist help in order to see Caddon's reign ended and his grip on the Eagle River country broken for ever.

It was late afternoon when Edge, with Gard Miller and his eight-man crew, hammered over the grasslands to reach Caddon's head-quarters. While they were still a half-mile out from the ranch buildings they spotted two riders drifting towards them. The pair rode at a leisurely enough pace until something told them that all was not well and that the men bearing down on them were not ordinary cowhands. Then they wheeled and sped back the way they had come.

'There'll be fireworks pretty soon,' Miller crowed at Edge's side. 'Wonder if Caddon'll see the writing on the wall and pack his hand.'

'I wouldn't bet on it,' Edge rejoined. He had difficulty containing the excitement that held him. Here at last was his chance to even the score for the death of his father. 'Get your men to spread out, Gard,' he said. 'If Caddon agrees to come to town and palaver, then well and good. If he doesn't, then we'll dicker in his own language.'

Oddly enough, there was no sign of life from the ranch buildings as the group scattered out and began to close in. By the time they had reached the front yard the steady advance had slowed to a walk. The air bristled with tension, with the potential for sudden violence. Edge went through the gateway and on into the yard. A chill settled at the base of his spine. He gestured to Gard Miller to hold his hand, then rode over to the porch.

He called: 'Caddon, come on out here with your hands up. Rimmel's dead. He tried to kill the sheriff, but Moze is alive. He's going to see you brought to trial.'

Silence rushed in when he had finished speaking. A breeze blew a couple of balls of tumbleweed up against the walls of the main building. Then a horse nickered somewhere round back. A dog emerged from an out-building, barked at the intruders, then raced away with its tail down.

'I don't like it much,' Miller whispered. He had the brim of his hat across his brow. His rifle poked over his saddle-horn.

'We'll try once more,' Edge decided. 'Caddon, if you don't come out right now we're going in to get you.'

That appeared to be the signal the Tumbling C boss was waiting for. A window along the porch was splintered and a Winchester barrel was stuck through. Edge saw Mark Caddon's face just before the cowman fired.

'Give them hell!' Caddon roared.

Edge's gun blasted at the window; he saw the rancher rock beneath his first shot and disappear. It was hard to believe that the boss of this cattle empire could be disposed of in this simple fashion. It had all been so easy to plan in the end, so easy to execute. Caddon's trouble was he had never envisaged the day when the tide might turn against him.

Gard Miller's men were off their horses now, racing to vantage points so that they might flush out the cowhands under siege. And suddenly it happened: they spilled from the barn and other outhouses. They tried to make a stand at the back of the main building. But their boss had gone down in that room and their hearts were no longer in the fight.

Edge scurried to the side of an upended wagon that had been relegated to the function of storing unwanted harness and other gear. He saw a man leap clear of the front door, poise on the porch, screech like a madman. Pinto Gahan with gun flaming.

Edge yelled: 'Pinto!'

Gahan brought his gun round, smoke and flame spurting from the muzzle. He was soon levelled to the porch duckboards by a withering hail of fire from Gard Miller's cowboys. Suddenly two of the Tumbling C faction broke and ran, hoping to find their horses and reach safety. They were cut down before they had covered a dozen feet.

Edge spotted Cash Mayne working his way over the roof of the main building, trailing a rifle. He unleashed two spaced shots and smiled grimly as Mayne levered up on his toes before pitching away into the back yard.

A tremendous pounding of hoofbeats approaching from the south brought Gard Miller ducking in beside Edge. At first they feared that more hardcases were coming to the aid of Tumbling C, but the dozen or so newcomers turned out to be a posse of townsmen led by Deputy Bob Lacey. The posse spread out around the ranch buildings as the last remnants of gunfire stuttered and faltered and then fell silent.

Edge quickly explained to the deputy all that had happened. Caddon's men were venturing into the open in two and threes, until there were ten of them rounded up and disarmed. Edge went into the house and found the room where he had seen Mark Caddon disappear below the window. The rancher's body lay on the floor, face down, the fingers of his right hand touched the stock of the rifle lying beside him.

Edge remained at the ranch for only a little while after that. He told Deputy Lacey and Gard Miller they could find him at Spanish Ridge. He would make arrangements for the wounded Moze Gall to be brought to town.

As he mounted the roan horse and pushed it out towards the open country he felt as if a great burden had been lifted from his shoulders. Whatever he and Barbie Wilson might decide to do at Spanish Ridge, there would be no Mark Caddon to cast a shadow across their future.

This Large Print Book, for people
who cannot read normal print,
is published under the auspices of

THE ULVERSCROFT FOUNDATION